TO TEMPT AN EARL

Lords of London, Book 3

TAMARA GILL

COPYRIGHT

KEEP IN CONTACT WITH TAMARA

Tamara loves hearing from readers and writers alike.
You can contact her through her website
www.tamaragill.com
or email her at tamaragillauthor@gmail.com.

DEDICATION

For my darling daughter, Lily.

CHAPTER 1

It was, without question, the worst week of Lord Hamish Doherty, Earl Leighton's life. He lay sprawled on the main floor of the Two Toads Inn, near the Berkshire border. His eyes watered as pain ricocheted through his face, blood pouring from his nose, that no amount of dabbing with his handkerchief would halt. So much for his unblemished profile, the ladies of the *ton* would be most upset to see that his nose was now a little crooked.

"I told ye, no matter who ye think ye are, if ye can't pay ye debt, I'll belt the money out of ye," the proprietor growled, his bulky frame distinctly menacing.

Hamish swiped at his nose, searching his pockets again for his purse, which was regretfully missing. Where the hell was it? He had it when he arrived three days past, had tipped the busty barmaid a gold coin after a very thorough servicing of his room, but after that his memory was hazy.

He'd gone for a ride yesterday to visit his good friend the Duke of Athelby at Ruxdon house, but with no need of funds there, he'd left his purse in the room. A stupid error of judgement considering the state his nose was now in.

Pushing away a surge of anger, he replied calmly, "This is merely a misunderstanding. I have funds. I left them in my room."

"Are ye saying that they've been stolen? That my inn is an establishment that allows such theft from those who stay under its roof?"

The publican wacked the wooden baton against his hand, a sure sign that would replace the fist that smacked into his nose a moment ago. Hamish looked about the room and cringed that he was now the centre of attention of other guests who were privy to his humiliation. No doubt he'd be the on dit all over town next week once they knew who he was. "Not necessarily...only that I had it when I left yesterday only to find it gone today. And I'm not saying that it was stolen, but only that it's missing, and *I* have not misplaced it."

The barmaid who he'd tupped huffed out an aggrieved breath. "Sounds like ye are trying to pin the stealing on one of us."

Hamish held up his hand when the publican took a step toward him. "I'm not, but I don't have the funds to pay for my debt. Let me send word to my friend, the Duke of Athelby and he'll pay the bill. I assure you." The publican narrowed his eyes and seemed a little less sure of his abuse at the mention of the duke, but it was only short-lived as he seemed to disregard Hamish's lofty contacts and took a threatening step toward him.

"Ye are a liar as well as a lout who cannot pay," the publican accused.

Damn, if there was anything Hamish disliked it was conflict, and he didn't wish to cause trouble so close to the Duke of Athelby's estate, but nor would he allow being treated so poorly. He was a peer, being beaten like a low life criminal. If the publican did not watch his future actions, he would find himself before the local magistrate for battery and theft.

"I'm the Earl Leighton. Do not confuse me for a lout without money or influence. If you come any closer to me with that bat, you'll find out quick enough just how true my words are."

The publican's eyes widened, and his advance stopped. Clearly the man was rethinking better of splitting Hamish's head open. "How do I know ye not lying about being a toff?"

A pair of sturdy boots came up to stand beside his head and he noticed they were well worn and a little dusty, probably from the inn yard. The gown that followed the boots was a dull, grey color, good for traveling. The face that glanced down at him was nothing short of angelic.

"How much does his lordship owe?" this mystery woman asked the publican, stepping between him and the man who'd already given him a bloody nose, which by the way, refused to stop bleeding. He pinched his nose harder.

"Four pounds will cover it, Miss Martin, and may I say how glad we are that ye are here to stay with us again."

She rummaged into her reticule and pulled out the correct amount, placing it into the publican's hand. "Have our luggage moved up to our rooms and have his lordship's carriage packed straight away. As for the gentleman's claims of being Lord Leighton, I can assure you he is who he says. I can vouch for him as we have mutual friends." She glanced at him quickly, her voice no-nonsense and calm. "I'm assuming since he was wanting to pay his account that his intentions were to leave."

"Of course, Miss Martin," the publican said, bowing and yelling out to the surrounding staff to do as she bade. "Apologies, my lord for any confusion. I hope you'll understand not knowing who ye were made me actions necessary."

Hamish glared at the bastard. "Let it be known I shall not shadow your establishment again, and nor will I ever recommend it."

Miss Martin kneeled beside him, holding out her gloved hand for him to take. He did, and she helped him to stand.

For a moment Hamish stared at the angel who'd saved his poor ass without his purse before she raised one, dark eyebrow.

"Lord Leighton, Miss Katherine Martin at your service. We've met before, at a ball I attended with my good friend Miss Cecilia Smith, now the Marchioness of Aaron."

Hamish frowned, racking his brain to place the beauty before him and came up blank. How could he forget such a woman? She appeared a lady who commanded authority and also had a backbone of steel. Even the hefty, large-boned publican didn't seem to faze her.

He met her piercing, intelligent brown orbs that were as dark as a rich coffee and his gut clenched. Upon standing one thing became perfectly clear, she was tall, almost as tall as him. She would never be regarded as a diamond of the first water, but Miss Martin was attractive. Her long, russet brown locks sat about her shoulders, neither tied back or accessorized with a bonnet. She stared at him with unwavering frankness, and as for her mouth, well, sensual and plump were two terms that came to mind...

"I'm embarrassed to say that I do not remember, but I'm very pleased to meet you and I thank you for your help today. I'm unabashedly ashamed of myself. I should have looked after my belongings better."

"I have no doubt that you've been stolen from, and yes, please when staying in such locales in the future, take better heed of your things. I may not always be about to save you." She threw him a grin and turned about on her heel, heading for the stairs.

"Wait!" he said, clasping her arm, gently urging her to face him once again, then releasing her. An inexplicable need to see her again welled inside him. A pretty blush had heated her cheeks possibly because of his familiarity, and he suppressed the urge to pull at his cravat like a schoolboy. "I must repay your kindness. We have mutual friends, shall I see you in town? How can I get in contact with you?" Hamish stopped saying anymore before he sounded like a desperate fool.

She rummaged in her reticule again, pulling out a small card. "We move in quite different social circles, even though my friend has married into the aristocracy. But perhaps we shall see each other again. As for repayment, should you or someone you know ever need a builder, please recommend my father's company. You'll not find more quality or better prices."

Hamish looked down at the card, it read: Mr. Montgomery Martin, Master Builder. "I hope we meet again, Miss Martin." No truer words had he said. She'd saved his hide, stepped in like an Amazonian warrior and fought off the evil publican. The need to meet again, not when he was bleeding like a stuck pig and dishevelled from being assaulted, burned though him. He wanted to see her again within his own sphere, his own terms. He would send a note to the Marchioness of Aaron on his return to London and see what she could arrange.

Miss Martin laughed, heading for the stairs. "Safe travels back to London, my lord. And please, remember my advice for the sake of that pretty nose of yours. I would hate for your bone structure to suffer any more ill effects from a fist."

A warm sensation tugged inside his chest. "So, you think I'm pretty, Miss Martin?"

"I believe I remarked only on your nose, my lord. Is it possible you are fishing for a compliment?"

Hamish chuckled and watched as the impudent, delightful miss walked up the stairs, the last image he had of her the little black boots as they stepped out of sight.

CHAPTER 2

Three months later…

Hamish hadn't thought life could get much worse after his sister's death. Her loss had cracked his heart open, and though echoes of grief still tormented him, a blessed numbness had wrapped his heart in a protective layer. A series of unfortunate incidents seemed determined to compound his misery and he truly hadn't thought anything could again stir his emotions which had been cauterized by pain. However, looking at the charred remains on what was left of a good portion of his London home, a home which had rung with happy memories of her joyous laughter, well, he had to amend such thoughts.

The year could bugger off for all he cared. First, he'd been assaulted at the Inn, the very Inn where his purse had been stolen. Upon arriving back in town he'd attended his favourite gaming hell, only to have been set upon by foot-pads where his winnings for the night, totalling almost a hundred pounds had been fleeced from him. He'd also suffered another bloody nose for his troubles.

Why he had been so unfortunate he could not fathom, unless the almighty was annoyed at him for not doing his duty and marrying a suitable young debutante. He was not looking to marry anytime soon if at all. His beloved sister's child would inherit his fortune and property, there was really no need for him to marry and reproduce at all. Even so, the amount of misfortune that had plagued him was starting to cause talk among his servants, and he no longer knew what to do to turn the tide back to being lucky instead of unlucky.

And now this. He shook his head, stepping back from the building when a large beam gave way, taking a portion of the floor with it. Servants and neighbors milled about him, looking up at what had once been part of his home. The part where he held his annual ball, and his sitting room on the first floor. All gone, nothing but ash and charred wood.

Damn it.

"I just heard, Hamish. I'm so sorry."

Hunter, the Marquess of Aaron, clapped him on the shoulder, holding him. "We'll have it rebuilt in no time. Do not despair."

Hamish wondered the time as the marquess was still dressed for his evening out, but there was no sign of Cecilia in the carriage. He sighed, not sure if he had it in him to take on such a task. He'd had so much bad luck of late, he'd likely have the job completed only to have it burnt down again. "Do you ever feel as though your life is wrong? That you must've done something so heinous, that the world is out to get you?"

Hunter looked at him. "No, but is that how you feel?"

Hamish grimaced. "I cannot help but feel that I need

to right some wrong or I'll continue to be somewhat cursed. No one I know has had as much misfortune as I have this year."

"You're talking about being attacked by footpads down in Vauxhall."

"Yes, but there have been other things as well." Maybe he'd not told Hunter all of what had happened to him since the death of his sister. Even so, it didn't change the fact that bad things continued to happen to him and he didn't know why. He was a rogue and a well sought-after gentleman yes, but he was not evil. He donated to the Duchess of Athelby and the Marchioness' of Aaron's London Relief Society every year. Paid his employees a fair wage and tried to be courteous to all, no matter their station. So, what was he doing wrong? Why did the fates of the world seem determined to have him crumble to his knees? It made no sense.

"You'd best be going. Cecilia will be wondering where you are, and I do not need to share my misfortune with others. It's probably best that you stayed away permanently."

"Do not take any heed of what the rumor mongers are saying about you."

Hamish rubbed a hand over his unshaven jaw. When the fire took hold last evening, he'd been abed and heard the cracking, popping sound coming from outside his door. Thank god he'd gone to investigate for he could've lost his whole home had he not alerted the servants and had two of them run and fetch the water engine while they fought with buckets of sand, water and sodden hessian bags.

"People are talking about me, and after this they will be even more so."

"Let us not worry about what has happened to you, but

what our next steps are in moving forward. You have to rebuild."

Which means he'll have to hire a master builder. The thought left him weary.

"You can stay with us until your home is repaired."

Hamish called over his steward who was inspecting the charred remains of his home. "Mr. Oakes, contact J Smith & Son lawyers and have them do an assessment for the insurance. We'll need to get this rebuild completed as soon as may be. We'll also need to hire two strong men to keep watch on the home until it is secure once again. I don't wish to lose anything else in this conundrum."

His agent bowed. "Yes, Sir. I'll get onto it right away."

"Henderson," Lord Aaron called out, gaining the attention of Hamish's valet who also stood on the street, his visage one of shock. "Pack up what you can of his lord-ship's clothing and have it sent around to my townhouse as soon as may be. Have Stubbs pack up whatever valuables he can manage. That'll have to do I'm afraid."

Hamish followed the marquess into the home to view the destruction more clearly, and although a lot of the building was smoke damaged, at least it was standing. How the remainder of the house hadn't caught alight was anyone's guess, but the thunder storm that came through, dousing the building with rain had helped. A little silver lining had been there at least. It was the reason the flames had been subdued and eventually put out. The charred walls, peeling, blackened wallpaper, family paintings that were smouldering was too much to take in, and within a few minutes Hamish strode toward the door. He couldn't look anymore. Tomorrow would be soon enough to deal with the mess.

"Sir, if you please before you depart," his steward said,

coming out of the room that had suffered serious damage due to the fire on the floor above.

"Yes, Mr. Oakes what is it?"

"I have sent for the insurance brokers and your lawyers. Stubbs and Henderson will bring everything that you asked for to the Marquess of Aaron's London home before luncheon tomorrow."

"Very good. I thank you," he said, eager to be away.

Their carriage waited down the lane a little way, due to the men who were already working on his home to secure it as best they could and to ensure the fire was definitely out. Hamish shook his head at the chaos this disaster had caused his neighbors and himself. To think only yesterday all was as it should be in Berkley Square and today, well, it was not what anyone would wish for.

Katherine sat at her desk in her father's library and read the missive from a Mr. Oakes, steward for the Earl of Leighton. She'd heard about the fire in Mayfair but hadn't know it was Lord Leighton who'd suffered the consequences.

She took out a piece of parchment and wrote Mr. Oakes, notifying him she would attend his lordship's home to commence a quote on the rebuilding of the wing that was damaged and that he could expect her by two in the afternoon.

"Everything well, my dear? I saw there were a few missives this morning."

Katherine glanced up to see her father poking his head about her door, his clothing was worn and dusty from the morning's job down at the south west dock on the Thames. His grey beard and bushy eyebrows also sported a little dust and she chuckled. No matter where he was, if he were in London he always ensured he came home to dine with her, especially after the loss of her mother only two years before. Whether he did it because he thought she was lonely, or he was, Katherine wasn't certain, but she enjoyed his company either way.

"We've been asked to quote up Lord Leighton's rebuild on his home on Berkeley Square. He was the gentleman who suffered from the fire last week. From what his man of business states, he lost a whole wing of his home. The entertaining part of his abode, so they're set on having it fixed as soon as may be."

"Entertaining part, hey?" her father said, grinning. "Did you not attend a ball there a year or so ago? With Cecilia?"

"I did," she said, standing and joining her father, taking his arm and leading him toward their dining room. "It was a lovely ballroom too. A great shame that it has been lost. They need a master builder and since you're by far the best in London, they've asked for you and no other."

"Well," her father said, standing a little taller by such praise. "I am honoured. Make sure when you go out on site that you are fair but honest, reasonable, but understanding. I should like to do another such project of such import, we have not had one for a year or so."

"No, we have not." They sat at the table, the smell of vegetable soup, warm and inviting filled the room as the first course was placed before them. This time of night, when it was just the two of them was Katherine's favourite. Since her mother's death the time they spent together talking about the events of their day had become religious.

They sat and started to eat, her father making complimentary noises with each spoonful of soup.

"What other rooms were damaged do you know?"

"The ballroom of course, part of an upstairs sitting room, the passage leading to these rooms has smoke damage and the roof in the ballroom has since collapsed, so it's all a rightful mess. But I'll take Thomas with me, and he'll measure up, make a detailed drawing of the rooms, such as they were, and we'll quote up after that.

"Do we know who'll be refurbishing the rooms?"

Katherine took her last sip of soup, laying down her spoon. "No, I have not been informed of that as yet, but I should imagine it'll be Mr. Hope who works with all those of Earl Leighton's calibre."

"Of course. I should've remembered."

The door to the dining room opened and in walked Katherine's cousin, her late mother's niece, Jane Digby. Katherine inwardly groaned. Since Jane had arrived a week past to enjoy the season with them, it had been seven days that Katherine was looking forward to putting behind her.

Jane, a pretty woman of nineteen had long blonde locks with just enough curl to add volume and enable styles to hold correctly. She wasn't too tall, like Katherine was, and her figure was pleasing. Worse was Jane knew she turned heads wherever she went with her bright blue eyes and flawless skin. Her only fault, her very bold, knowing speech. Maybe due to the fact that living in the small country parish near Nottingham didn't allow for her to learn what one should and should not discuss. It was no error of the girl, her mother obviously lavished attention with little restraint, but now the result of such laxity in her upbringing meant Katherine made every effort to avoid her since Jane and her lofty opinions now included all of Katherine's faults. What she could wear that would bring out the color of her eyes better, or help in hiding her almighty height that was not favourable to men of their class. Or what she could do with her hair to help conceal the dull brown she'd been born with.

"Oh, I'm so sorry I'm late. I wanted your maid, Mary to do my hair. She's so very clever, but it took an age to complete." Jane sat at the table, and placing a napkin on her lap, gestured for the footman to serve her the soup course.

"It looks lovely, my dear," her father said, catching Katherine's eyes, a twinkle of mirth in his.

"Where did you find the feather?" Katherine took a sip of wine, anything to stop her lips from grinning at the girl's exuberant hair style.

Jane ate her soup, nodding eagerly. "Oh yes, I wanted a peacock's feather, but I could only find one from an old hat in the attic. I think it may be a chicken feather."

Her father coughed, and Katherine took pity on her cousin. "We shall go down to the haberdashers tomorrow and we'll see if we can find you more suitable feathers for your hats. What do you think of that?"

Jane literally bounced in her chair, her eyes bright with excitement. "Oh, how I should love to do that. And maybe while we're there they may have a hat for you to replace the one you use on our walks in the park each day. Your hair is such a bland, dull colour of brown and your bonnet being of the same color does nothing for you. If you're to catch a husband, you really ought to put more effort into your appearance."

Katherine smiled, thanking the footman as he served her the second course. "Thank you, Jane. I shall take your advice into consideration," she said with forced politeness, not wanting to snap at Jane's inconsiderate remarks and cause an argument that would distress her father.

"Oh, you should," Jane continued, pushing away her soup and asking for the second course. "All my friends in

Gotham tell me I'm an expert on these things and they do everything that I tell them. You should. I would lay a wager that should you take all my advice you'll gain a husband sooner rather than later."

"If Katherine gains a husband, I lose a daughter. Do not rush into anything my dear. I should miss you."

Katherine smiled at her father, having no intention of gaining a husband, not unless they were ideal ones like her two good friends, Marchioness of Aaron or the Duchess of Athelby. The Marquess and Duke were the best of men, possessing qualities she wanted in her own union. They were loving and caring toward their wives, and Cecilia coming from the same stock as Katherine, so much lower in society than his lordship only made him worthier of her friend's love. To put what Society expects of him aside and marry for love ensured Katherine adored him almost as much as Cecilia did.

"Are you attending Cecilia's card night tonight, my dear? Unless I'm mistaken and it's a different day altogether."

Katherine pulled her mind away from her musings of her friends' happy marriages or the fact that she'd once longed for something similar. To have a family and children, but now at six and twenty, those dreams seemed ever more distant with each day. "I am, papa. I'll be leaving after dinner."

"In that gown?" Jane asked, assessing the gown , distaste clouding her inspection.

She looked down at her light pink muslin dress. Although not the height of fashion, it was pretty and not damaged or marked. After all, it was only a card night with close friends, not like a ball where Katherine would be expected to dress in the heights of fashion.

"What is wrong with this dress? I thought it suited me very well."

"You look beautiful, my dear," her father stated, pushing away his second course.

"It's so plain and boring. Why, you positively look drab."

"Jane, that is unkind," her father put in with a frown.

At her father's response, Jane turned her attention to her meal. Their quiet repast didn't last long.

"I didn't mean to be mean, uncle. I merely wish for Katherine to do well when she's out at parties and events. Should my cousin gain a good marriage, it would improve my own prospects. I would loathe having to marry a country clergyman. How awful that should be. I'm sure I should die of boredom within the first month."

If only they were so lucky... "Tonight's event is merely a friendly get together and I can assure you, my gown, as plain and dull as it is, will do very well. My friends do not care what I wear, so long as I attend." Katherine stood, coming around and kissing her father's cheek. "I shall leave you now. I asked for the carriage to be out front by seven and it's almost time."

Her father patted her arm. "Very good my dear. I shall see you when you return home."

"I may be late. Do not wait up."

Katherine headed out into the foyer, slipping on her bonnet before picking up her cloak and gloves where she'd left them near the front door. As expected her carriage sat waiting for her. Leaning against the cushioned squabs, she sighed in relief being away from her cousin. As much as she cared for the girl, she was best served in little doses. Her constant criticism of her person was wearing. Katherine didn't need anyone to tell her of her faults. She knew them very well.

She was a woman who worked for her father, managed most things other than the manual labor her father's building company was known for. A tall woman, she was too thin, too lanky to be attractive. A Long Meg as some called her. Not to mention small breasts made her look like a stick. Katherine looked down at her bodice and tried to adjust her gown to give her the appearance of more cleavage. She sighed, giving up when her efforts accomplished nothing. There was no hope, she was what she was and there was nothing she could do about it.

The carriage pulled up before Cecilia's home, and Katherine jumped down without help. The front door opened, and Cecilia's butler smiled in welcome.

"Miss Martin, please come inside. The marchioness is waiting for you in the drawing room."

"Thank you, Thomas." Katherine handed him her cloak and started toward the hall beside the stairs. The home was bright with light and smelt of flowers. Since Cecilia had married the Marquess last spring, she'd taken to having floral arrangements in every room no matter the season, and the home smelt divine always.

Katherine smiled as a footman opened the door for her into the drawing room and she entered to a room full of people, laughing and playing cards. A woman sat playing at the piano-forte, there was more in attendance than she had thought to be, and Jane's reminder of her gown made her stomach drop. Perhaps she should have changed into something more fitting.

"You're here," Cecilia said, making her way through the guests, and reaching Katherine, pulled her into a fierce hug. "I'm so glad you came. I need someone I can really talk to." Cecilia wore a striking cerulean blue silk gown that flowed over her like water. Her friend had such beautiful clothes these days that she couldn't help but feel a little jealous over her remarkable sense of style.

"You can talk to me," the marquess said, coming to stand beside them.

Katherine laughed, and Cecilia smirked. "You know what I mean," she said.

"Luckily I do," the marquess said. He turned to Katherine and leaning down, kissed her cheek. "We have not seen enough of you, Kat. You need to visit us more often. Thank you for coming tonight."

Cecilia took Katherine's arm, pulling her into the room. "Come and sit by me and Darcy. We're discussing what we're going to do this Season and we want you to be involved as well. As much as your father can spare you, of course. We know you're very busy."

The thought of working each day, and now with the possibility of Lord Leighton's home rebuild, didn't leave much room for socializing. Though if she was to find a husband as loving and sweet as the duchess and marchioness did, well, then she'd have to put her need for sleep aside and do what she must. Dance until dawn. She loved her papa and loved working with him, but she still yearned for the fulfilment of a husband and children someday.

Her parents' marriage had been such a happy one, full of love and respect. Growing up she'd been supported and unconditionally loved, and wanted the same for her own children if she were so fortunate.

"What did you have in mind?"

The Duchess welcomed her with a warm hug also, and before long it had been an hour of nothing but chatter about gowns, balls and parties. The duchess was looking forward to holding a country visit mid-season at their estate in Berkshire. All of which Katherine was invited to should she wish to attend.

A slight tittering from the ladies who stood about the room caught Katherine's attention and she turned to see Lord Leighton enter, standing in the threshold and surveying them all like a sitting god looking over his mere mortals. Katherine had seen him before, a few times in fact considering they had mutual friends, but tonight dressed in light colored satin knee-breeches and a long-tailed blue superfine coat he was beyond perfect. He appeared like he was attending the grandest ball in London.

Not cards and drinks with friends.

"I am here!" he declared, laughing and walking over to the Duke of Athelby and the Marquess who stood aside of the guests talking. The men shook hands and Katherine watched them, unable to tear her eyes away from Lord Leighton and his lovely, extraordinary male form.

Not that she should be looking at men in this society, certainly not in the way she was regarding Lord Leighton, but it was hard to not admire their dashing elegance. No men should be born with such beauty and his lordship had that in droves. Unlike most men of his set, Lord Leighton had long hair, or at least, shoulder length. His locks were tied back in a black ribbon tonight, and the design brought out his cutting cheekbones and generous lips. As for his eyes, they were his finest feature if she had to pick one, and in all honestly there were many to choose from. But his eyes were almond in shape and were such a dark shade of onyx that they were almost black. She inwardly sighed at his beauty, marvelling how anyone could be born with not only wealth and stature but also looks. How lucky he was.

"Have you met, Lord Leighton?" the duchess asked, sitting back in the chair and flicking a glance in the direction of her husband.

"I have. And tomorrow I'm to meet with him in relation to supplying his man of business with a quote for the rebuild of his home. What a terrible situation for him to be in. Do you know where he's staying while his home is repaired?"

"He's staying here," Cecilia said, matter of fact. "Will be here for some time from what I understand. The damage was substantial and will take some months to repair."

"It is very bad, but it could've been a lot worse. It was lucky he woke up and was able to sound the alarm, or he could've been killed," Katherine added.

"Very true." The duchess smiled, as her husband came to stand beside her.

"Miss Martin, have you met Lord Hamish Doherty, Earl Leighton," the duke said, gesturing to his friend as he came to join them. The Marquess of Aaron following close and went to stand behind Cecilia.

Katherine met the Earls eyes and saw the moment he recognized her.

"Well, what chance is this? The lady who saved my life. How do you do, Miss Martin. I hope you're enjoying your evening?"

"I am, thank you, my lord. And I must say I'm glad to see that you made it back to London after all, although I am sad to hear about the fire you've suffered this past week."

"Thank you, yes. As you can see I'm back in town, thanks to you."

"Why do I get the feeling you two have a little story that we're not aware of." The duchess said, glancing back and forth between them.

"Because we do," the Earl said, matter of fact, before taking a sip of his champagne. "Miss Martin saved my hide at an inn on my way home from your estate in fact. And I have not forgot your kindness, my dear. I still owe you."

"And you shall owe her more after tomorrow," Cecilia added, grinning.

The Earl frowned. "Why is that?" he asked.

Katherine took pity on the man. "You may have forgotten, but I believe I mentioned that my father is a master builder, my lord. I'm to meet with your man of business tomorrow to quote for the structural repairs to your home here in London."

"You?" the Earl said, his brow raised in obvious shock.

"Careful, Hamish, remember you're surrounded by three very strong women right at this moment," the duke said, smiling.

"I meant no offence, Miss Martin, I'm just shocked that is all. I did not think women partook in such employment."

"Normally they do not, but I'm the exception," she said with a small smile, pride warming her chest. And tomorrow she would prove to him exactly how much of an exception she was. Her mind was quick, and her mathematical skills better than most, as was her ability to barter for the best wood prices one could get in London and beyond. It was why her father trusted and relied on her so much in the business. Between them they checked, and double checked their calculations and sums and they were yet to make a mistake, hence why they were so very busy.

The Earl's direct gaze caressed over her length and a peculiar shiver stole over her. Did he like what he saw or was he merely curious that the woman across from him wasn't the standard so many of his ilk married?

She didn't need her cousin Jane to remind her of her lack of charm and elegance. Around the duchess and

Cecilia, it was no secret she lacked their beauty and social confidence. Katherine was from trade, quite literally, a builder's daughter and one who worked in the company. And although Cecilia, a woman from her social sphere had married a marquess, she was at least considered not as rough about the edges as Katherine since she hailed from a barrister's family.

Katherine took in her gown and compared it to her friends. Their elegant silk, the cut and design of their dresses were the height of fashion, made her own modest dress look as cheap as it was compared to theirs.

Lifting her chin, she took a sip of her wine and fought to push the self-doubt aside. Darcy and Cecilia were her friends and would never ostracize her, no matter what Society might like to do.

Life was passing her by, her friends were starting families and marrying, while she seemed to be stuck, never moving forward, except towards old age.

"I look forward to viewing your quote, Miss Martin. Pleasure to meet you again," Lord Leighton said, bowing before going off to join another set of guests. They welcomed him with laughter and perfect curtsies and his absence was missed.

Katherine watched him for a moment before turning her attentions back to her friends. Men like Lord Leighton didn't see women like her as equals. Not wealthy or connected enough, and now at six and twenty her prospects of actually marrying at all, even in her own social sphere seemed a lost dream. As she grew older, Katherine had to admit that she didn't seem to belong anywhere, except at her work. She was doomed to die an old maid. A woman who'd never experienced a stolen kiss or a wicked embrace from men of Lord Leighton's ilk. Or anyone's for that matter.

As the night wore on, as the card games and music started with impromptu dancing, and no gentleman asked her to dance, the little demoralizing sound of Jane's voice wouldn't abate. It's constant reminding that she didn't belong, wasn't wanted and was not refined enough for her friends wouldn't quieten.

No matter how much she told herself it was not so.

CHAPTER 3

K atherine stood with Mr. Andrew Perry, their foreman outside Earl Leighton's home and tapped her pencil against her notepad. The lord was over an hour late and still there was no sign of an arriving carriage or gentleman heading toward his home on foot.

"Maybe we ought to come back another time, Miss Katherine. His lordship seems to have forgotten."

Katherine looked up and down the street again and frowned. "It is odd that his man of business hasn't even arrived. I see there are men inside cleaning up, maybe if we start the measuring up and do the inspection his lordship will arrive afterwards. There may have been some kind of time mix up."

Andrew harrumphed, but followed as she walked up the townhouse steps, entered the entrance hall where a flurry of workers stood, some upstairs and others working on the room beneath where the fire took hold.

"We'll start upstairs and work our way down."

Just then the front door opened and in walked a hurried Mr. Oakes, a sheen of sweat covering his face, his hair sticking up on end as if he'd been running. "Mr. Perry, Miss Martin, I presume."

Katherine held out her hand and the man shook it, before shaking Mr. Perry's as well.

"I do apologize. His lordship had stated he wished to attend today but sent me a note that arrived only half an hour past that he'd changed his mind. I was not prepared and knew you would already be waiting, and so I'm terribly late. I am most sorry."

Katherine smiled, trying to put the harried man at ease. "No need to concern yourself. Shall we begin?" It did not surprise her that Lord Leighton didn't wish to see her again or discuss his repairs with a woman. After their initial conversation last evening, he'd gone off and practically twirled about the room, talking to any and all female guests Cecilia had invited, gushing over them, and making all of them blush and giggle like little nincompoops.

It only proved yet again that she was plain and unbecoming and not a woman that would ever turn Lord Leighton's head. He was a man who oozed charm and spectacular looks, while she oozed trade and little appeal at all.

A pity, she had anticipated seeing him. Perhaps it was for the best, for what good could come of any interaction outside of business matters?

"This way, if you please," Mr. Oakes said, starting up the stairs.

Katherine followed and over the next hour they measured, discussed wood, took samples of what was there, and Katherine drew the layout of the room, the structure of the ceiling, or at least what was left of it.

Katherine felt for his lordship having lost one of the grandest ballrooms in London, but at least one of its greatest features being the marble fireplace had survived, even if it was a little discoloured by smoke.

Mr. Oakes explained what the Earl expected with regard to the rebuild and what changes he wished to make, the largest being a terrace that came off the ballroom and considering the ballroom was on the first floor of this home, it would take a little design and consideration to have this put in place. But it was no hardship for her father to do, and when all the building work was completed, Lord Leighton would be satisfied, just as all their customers were.

With their business complete, she turned to Mr. Oakes and held out her hand. "Good day, sir. Thank you for your assistance and input. We'll have a quote ready for his lordship by Monday next week."

He took her hand, shaking it. "Thank you, Miss Martin. You've been very professional. Give my regards to your father."

They left and climbed up in their waiting carriage, telling the driver to return to the office.

A pleased smile crossed Mr. Perry's lips. "I think that went well. Your thoughts, Miss Martin?"

"I agree, and I think after seeing the damage, that should his lordship choose us for the rebuild we should have him back in his home within six months, if the weather is favourable."

"Has his lordship decided on who'll refurbish the home, we should probably consult with them before we commence."

"I will send word to his man of business, I don't know why I forgot to ask him today. But even so, should he not know, I shall ask Lord Leighton directly. He is staying at my good friend's home, the Marchioness of Aaron." And she was to dine with them the following Saturday, just a select few of friends, which Katherine assumed to be the duke and duchess of Athelby. If Lord Leighton attended she would ask him then. Settling back on the squabs, Katherine pushed away the little flutter that took flight in her stomach at the thought of seeing his lordship again.

There was no point in her dreaming about him, he would never look to her for a wife or a dalliance even. Too plain, too common to turn anyone of his sets' eyes, but even so, it didn't mean she couldn't look at him, take her fill and enjoy daydreaming about what his soft looking lips would feel like against hers.

She sighed. *I bet they would feel wickedly good…*

"Did you say something, Miss Martin?"

Katherine shook her head. "I was just mumbling to myself. Please ignore me." Just dreaming of things she'd love to have, even if for a moment, but might never experience. The fact that Lord Leighton didn't even bother to show up for their appointment today told her all she needed to know where he ranked her importance in his life. Why she was so invisible to people other than her friends baffled her. She had a good dowry, wasn't beautiful she would admit, but nor was she unattractive, so it had to be due to her uninspiring figure. And the fact she worked for a living. Perhaps Jane was right and she needed to upgrade her wardrobe and purchase a new hat. Anything to mix it up a little, make her appear to have all the appearance of a lady who knew how to dress, how to attract men, when really, she had no idea at all.

HAMISH GLANCED across the dining table at the marquess of Aaron's home and slowly chewed the roasted chicken he was eating while trying to figure out Miss Martin who sat across from him. Her mind was as quick as any man's he'd ever known, her intelligence and knowledge on news and current affairs was better than his own he also admitted. By all appearances she was a modern, educated woman. But her gown, it was at least two seasons old, and although her hair was tidy, it did little to bring out her dark, alluring eyes.

Did she dress with so little care to hide the becoming, charming visage, or maybe she simply did not care for the fripperies that so many women of his class lived to purchase.

For him, he loved seeing women dressed in the latest fashions, their hair bejewelled and a little rouge on the lips made one long to smudge it across their mouth in a passionate kiss. When Miss Martin had saved his nose from further damage at the inn some months past, he'd not thought to see her again, but he also hadn't forgotten that he owed her a small debt of gratitude.

And now after seeing her father's building company's quote, a very reasonable one considering they were the best in London, he would be seeing a lot more of her in the coming months since he'd decided to use them. For reasons even he didn't know, he would like to see her again. Talk to her more. Find out what her passions and pursuits were and see if this wallflower before him would blossom into a rose.

Hamish cleared his throat. "I wished to tell you, Miss Martin that I've decided to hire your father to rebuild my home. I know it is crass to talk business at events such as these, but my man of business spoke highly of you and Mr. Perry's professionalism and the quote was very reasonable. When do you think you shall be able to start?"

The duchess clapped, smiling. "Oh, I'm so glad you've chosen to go with Mr. Martin, Hamish. You shall not be disappointed. He's helped us with all our building works we've taken part in with the Orphanages and schools. Katherine and her father are simply the best."

A light blush stole over Katherine's cheeks making her even a little more handsome than Hamish thought possible. She was not the type of woman he would normally ever glance at, not because of her rank or clothing, he wasn't an idiot, but simply she was so very lithe and tall. He loved nothing more than a woman with a little curve to her, a woman who held the shape of the female form. He was, to put it bluntly, a man who adored breasts and bottom of equal size.

Miss Martin, although not completely unfortunate in relation to her breasts, had a good handful at most, but not much more.

He took a sip of wine when her gaze met his. "Thank you, Lord Leighton. I'm very happy to hear this and shall tell papa the good news on my return home tonight."

He grinned, amused by her proper speech to him. With everyone else she was carefree, laughing and involving herself without second thought, but with him, she was a little guarded, careful with her words and it made him wonder.

"Katherine, I forgot to ask you last week, but we've all been invited to the O'Callaghan's ball and we hoped you would attend with us. I shall have the carriage sent around to pick you up and then we shall all travel together from there. It is Thursday next," Cecilia interjected.

Again, she confounded Hamish. At the mention of a ball her eyes brightened and without qualm he could term Katherine a beauty. When she wished to be and wasn't hiding under dowdy clothes.

"Thursday next? I shall have to check with papa that

we have no outstanding engagements, but I'm sure it'll be fine."

"There is supposed to be good gaming, Hamish. Are you attending?" the duke asked, pushing his dessert away. Lord Aaron called for the port, and the ladies stood, signalling the end of the meal.

"I will be. I promised Lady O'Callaghan that I would dance the first waltz with her and I should hate to disappoint her ladyship."

"Be careful, Hamish or you'll find yourself betrothed to her ladyship right smart. You know as well as all of us, that she's after a new husband after her last one died under unfortunate circumstances." The duchess said, chuckling.

"I would think dying under any circumstance would be unfortunate," Katherine said, matter of factly.

Cecilia placed her napkin on the table, nodding. "The duchess meant Kat that her ladyship's husband died under her ladyship when they were within their private apartment."

"Well, poor man, or maybe, lucky man depending on which way you look at it," Katherine said, chuckling.

Hamish shut his mouth with a snap having never heard a woman speak so openly and about that particular subject in polite Society. His past mistresses had sometimes spoken with such candor and little regard to those about them, but never had he seen it take place within his own Society. Men, yes, very often spoke in such ways, but women, never. The duke and marquess laughed and Hamish too found himself amused and not a little intrigued by her.

The ladies stood, and Hamish's gaze followed Miss Martin...*Kat* out the door before a footman closed it, leaving just himself, the duke and marquess alone.

"Do the ladies always talk in such ways? I say, I've never heard Cecilia ever say such things in polite Society."

Hunter chuckled. "Those three women are the best of friends and I shudder to think what they discuss when we're not around. I'm sure Katherine knows all about married life, and what happens between a man and woman in the marriage bed. To hear them speak so at table, around friends, is nothing to them."

"A quite common occurrence I should say," the marquess added. "Why the other day I heard Cecilia telling Kat about the rumors circulating the *ton* regarding Lord Leslie and his valet."

"What rumors? I've not even heard this one." Hamish looked from both men, wondering when they had become so, so *married*! He leaned back in his chair, taking a cigar when the duke offered him one. "What do you think of Miss Martin?"

Both men turned steely gazes on him and Hamish took a long pull of his smoke, wondering what exactly was going through their minds right at this moment. His mind was filled with thoughts of a woman he had no right to be thinking of at all. He didn't even want a wife.

"She is lovely, and we care for her as much as Darcy and Cecilia would care for a sister should they have one, and so, when you ask what we think of her, we wonder what you mean by such a query, Hamish," the duke said, raising one brow and looking quite severe.

It reminded Hamish of what the duke looked like before he married Darcy, stern and ill-tempered. Hamish paused, wondering himself what he meant. He rubbed his jaw, contemplating his words. "Miss Martin is polite, and well mannered, but she lacks refinement that the duchess and marchioness both exhibit. I know Cecilia and Katherine grew up beside one another in Cheapside and look at each other like sisters, but it is odd now that Cecilia is a marchioness that their friendship is still as strong."

Hunter leaned forward in his chair, putting out his cigar in the tray provided. "Why would their friendship not continue? Kat is wonderful, and I would never suggest to Cecilia to cease such a friendship."

"You must admit, she is getting on in years, and is yet to be married. Not to mention her clothes, her hair. And she's to attend lord and lady Keppel's ball with you all next week. What will she wear! I fear to find out. It is a little peculiar, you must admit." Hamish leaned back in his chair, picturing Miss Martin in an embroidered silk gown in a deep, rich color. She would be as beautiful as any woman he'd known. He frowned. Where the hell did that thought come from.

The duke shrugged. "I like Miss Martin and would never wish to exclude her in any way. I grant you her clothes are not the most fashionable, nor her hair the most styled, but she is loyal, honest and kind. And Darcy loves her, and then, so too do I. I hope this is not going to be a problem for you, Hamish. She is our friend, and I do not want you to injure her pure soul just because she's not as fashionable and rich as so many of your friends are."

At his silence Hunter glanced at him. "Hamish? Do we have a problem?"

Hamish threw his cigar into the fire, standing. "Of course not. I merely thought it odd, is all. But if you wish her to be part of your set in our society, who am I to naysay that. Even if she is the builder of my home I shall be obliged to dance with her at balls."

Hunter laughed. "I shall hold you to that, and you never know, you may enjoy your dance with Miss Martin. She may charm you as much as she's charmed all of us."

"Perhaps," he said, heading for the door that a footman opened for them. "But for now, I shall bid you all goodnight. I have a card game to attend and a buxom lady friend who wishes for her own private dance with me."

The duke shook his head as Hamish took his cloak and hat from the footman in the hall. "See you at the ball, Hamish. And remember to bring your best manners with you."

He clasped his chest in mock insult. "Of course. When have I ever been otherwise?"

Hamish was soon settled into his carriage and looking out the window he thought of his friends, their love match marriages and how lucky they were. He'd once thought such a life was what he'd wanted, but after the death of his sister, the pain it caused his family and that of her husband he was no longer so sure. To lose someone again he loved seemed an idiotic thing to do. To put one's feelings on the line, be vulnerable wasn't what he wanted for himself.

His nephew would inherit his title, he didn't need to marry if he didn't wish to settle with a lady. His life was full, he wasn't short of bed partners, and the entertainments of his set kept him busy. The image of Katherine Martin floated through his mind, of being greeted at home by a woman of her lively intelligence and prettiness, having her warm his bed and no one else, and he wondered at his course in life.

Wondered if his life of idleness was what he really wanted.

CHAPTER 4

"It is too much, your grace. I couldn't possibly wear such a masterpiece." Katherine slid her hand along the golden silk gown with an abundance of silver silk embroidery and decorated with hundreds of glass beads and silk cording. Never had she seen such a beautiful dress and picking it up she held it before her in the looking glass, surprised the color suited her.

"You will look beautiful, and since you're staying here this evening, I shall not take no for an answer. I'll have my maid do your hair, and you'll be the prettiest lady at the Leeders' annual ball." Darcy rang the bell for a servant in the pretty little room she'd allocated her. A single bed covered in a blue floral design complimented the blue velvet drapes across the bank of windows. A small chaise sat at the end of the bed and considering the size of the room it allowed one to warm themselves before the well stoked fire.

"You're being too nice, but truly, I'll feel odd wearing something that suits people of your sphere more than mine. Won't people look at me as a fraud?"

Darcy sent the footman who she was talking to at the door away with orders to bring up a hip bath and turned to her with a small frown across her brow.

"I don't ever wish to hear you say such a thing again. You're the duchess of Athelby and marchioness of Aaron's closest friend. No one would dare look down on you in any other way other than pure adoration. And if they do not, they will have me to face."

Darcy came over and clasped her hand, squeezing it a little. "Some people are not born into privilege such as I was, and some marry into this life, such as Cecilia has, but it does not make anyone anywhere else any less worthy of respect or cordiality. We are all humans after all. I do not want you to feel like you're lesser than us for you are not." Darcy took the gown from her and laid it on the bed. "If I have made you feel like you would be uncomfortable in this gown, you are of course free to wear whatever you like, and I shall stand beside you, just as proud as I would should you be wearing nothing at all."

Katherine chuckled, and went to stand before the dress. Oh, it was so very pretty, so very heavy and would've had hundreds of sewing hours in the creation of it. "I merely worry that people will think I'm trying to be someone I'm not. But," she said, sighing, admiring the gown yet again.

"You're right. What should I care what people think or believe, it is only a gown." Katherine turned to Darcy. "I shall wear it, and I shall enjoy every moment I'm in such a beautiful masterpiece. Thank you for allowing me this little luxury."

Darcy clapped her hands just as a light knock sounded on the door. "Kat, the night will be so much fun, and you will look utterly stunning." Darcy bade the servants enter and a footman carried in a hip bath along with a bevy of other servants who brought up steaming buckets of hot water. A maid left her linens and lavender soap on a chair beside the bath.

"I shall leave you now, my dear, and will see you after you're dressed. Ring the bell when you're ready for your hair to be dressed and my maid will attend you. I shall see you in the entrance hall by eight."

THE LEEDERS' ball was a crush and Katherine followed the duke and duchess into the ballroom after they were introduced at the door. If it felt as though hundreds of eyes had turned her way she was not far off. Looking about the room, a lot of the *haute ton* glanced in her direction, some curious no doubt on whom the duke and duchess had brought while others, those that had seen her at other events looked down their nose at her even being in their presence.

Katherine raised her chin and came to stand beside Darcy as a footman carrying a tray of champagne stopped before them. Katherine picked up a flute and took a well needed sip. "There are so many people here this evening. How will we find Cecilia in this crush?"

The duchess craned her neck, looking about and nodding in acknowledgment to those who tried to gain her attention. "Cecilia and Hunter will be along soon, and I told her I would be in this situation in the ballroom, so she should find us well enough."

Lady Oliver, who had been traveling abroad with her husband Viscount Oliver waved to the duchess and made a direct line toward them. The duchess smiled, clearly pleased that her friend who'd been away from town for the past eighteen months was back among them.

"Fran," the duchess said, kissing her friend on both cheeks before they embraced quickly. "I'm so happy to see you again." She kissed the viscount and then turned them to where Katherine and the duke were waiting.

"Athelby you know, but let me introduce you to my new friend, Miss Katherine Martin. She grew up with Lady Aaron, as you may remember me telling you in my letters."

Lady Oliver smiled at Kat and she had the impression she was genuinely happy to meet her finally. She let the few nervous knots dissipate in her stomach that had lodged there wondering if the duchesses' friend wouldn't approve of her.

Katherine bobbed a curtsy. "It's lovely to meet you, Lady Oliver. I understand you've been traveling abroad and have seen even the pyramids of Egypt."

Her ladyship smiled, clearly remembering the wonderful sights she'd visited. "We did, and they were the most wonderful of places. And I almost forgot to tell you Darcy, but I found the most amazing woman while traveling there. Her name is Lady Georgina Savile, a widow of great fortune, and she'll be arriving in London by month's end. Lord Oliver and myself are going to be holding a ball in her honor and you must simply come, you too, Miss Martin, if you wish to."

"I should be honoured to attend," Katherine said, delighted to be included. The conversation turned to the other sites the viscountess' had seen over her many months abroad and Katherine took the opportunity to watch the dancers and other guests.

On the dance floor a flash of scarlet caught her eye and looking, spotted Earl Leighton dancing with a blonde woman in a deep red silk gauze gown and silk trim that sat over a white muslin gown. The gown was so becoming on the woman, and her figure highlighted every pretty little feature and silk design that sat across the bodice.

Katherine's enjoyment of the ball dimmed a little at seeing Lord Leighton so entranced by the woman who had curves that perfectly accentuated the woman's form. It shouldn't surprise Katherine that she would not turn his head. One needed to be a siren to capture the beautiful and popular Lord Leighton.

The night passed and soon it was after midnight and still no one other than the duke and the marquess of Aaron had asked her to dance. Not even the pretty gown her friend had given her to use could persuade men to ask her to step out with them.

Katherine tried to include herself into her friends' conversations as much as she could, but as the night crept further into the early hours of the morning, it became harder and harder. She'd been up early the day of the ball to check the delivery of the hardwoods that were to be used at Lord Leighton's home, and she'd had a meeting with Mr. Perry and his lordship's man of business Mr. Oakes to discuss the week's progress and what was to go forward the next. Her presence at a ball, when it was well past her retiring time, left her eyes heavy and her feet aching, even in slippers that felt like she was walking on air.

The mention of Lord Leighton's name caught her attention and she looked up from inspecting her champagne glass to see his lordship walking over to them. This time a different woman from the one in scarlet she'd seen him dancing with earlier in the night. This woman had striking auburn hair, tied up in in a motif of curls and a delicate strand of diamonds threaded throughout. Her gown was almost ebony in colour with gold thread in decorative flowers around the hem, bodice and sleeves.

Katherine gritted her teeth, not wanting to believe his

lordship was so obsessed with beauty as he seemed to be. She was a fool to have even thought of him in any other way more than as a mutual acquaintance.

"Lord Leighton, how good of you to drag yourself away from your entertainments to come speak with us," the duchess of Athelby said, giving him her hand to kiss.

He bowed and introduced his guest to them all. A Lady Scottle, wife of the late Baron Scottle.

His lordship's gaze moved over them all but stopped on her, his eyes widening as he took in her appearance. She raised her chin, readying herself for whatever he was about to say. The last thing she wanted him to think was she was dressing up to impress his set. It was the last thing she was doing, no matter what she wore, she would never succumb to changing who she was.

"Miss Martin?" he asked, stepping toward her and dropping Lady Scottle's arm who merely went to stand beside Darcy and Cecilia and started to chat.

Katherine bobbed a curtsy. "Lord Leighton, I hope you're enjoying the ball."

His attention flicked over her again and warmth speared through her stomach as his eyes heated appreciatively. She'd seen disappointment often reflected in others, and duty by gentleman when they'd done the right thing and danced with her. But in this case, the reaction on Lord Leighton's face wasn't anything she'd ever seen before. Certainly not at her. She'd seen appreciation and desire bestowed on others, but she'd never been pretty enough to warrant such sincere admiration.

It would seem a beautiful gown and a little rouge on one's lips could do wonders.

"Is that really you?" he said, picking up her hand and bowing over it. "How beautiful you look this evening."

Katherine took back her hand when he forgot to let it

go and smiled to quell the butterflies taking flight in her stomach. "It is me, merely dressed a little more appropriately for the occasion."

"Gold suits you," he said, staring at her with what Katherine hoped was awe.

The lady he'd walked over to their group with came up to him and slid her arm through his lordship's. A very familiar gesture if Katherine had ever seen one. "Dance with me, Hamish. It's to be a waltz."

Katherine stepped back to give them privacy and started when Lord Leighton clasped her hand, placing it onto the crook of his arm. "Forgive me, Lady Scottle but I'd already promised this dance to Miss Martin."

The duchess stepped in and pulled her ladyship over toward where she was speaking with Cecilia. Katherine walked out onto the floor with his lordship, masking her shock that his lordship had just lied to a woman. Fibbed most believably and worse she'd allowed him to, just so she could dance with him.

He swung her into his arms and she met his gaze, trying not to get lost in the beautiful vision that was Lord Leighton. "You just fibbed, my lord. To a woman who did not expect you to ask another woman right in front of her to dance. Are you always so flippant?"

His lordship grinned, his gloved hand warm about hers. His touch upon her hip made her conscious of the fact that she wasn't as rounded and womanly as the lady he'd left with their friends. Her figure although thin, and pleasant enough, wasn't soft womanly curves, or as bountiful in some regions as all men liked. Or so she'd heard...

"I think that is the wrong word and unless you tell Lady Scottle she will never know the truth of the matter. And anyway, I wished to dance with you."

"Why?" she asked, truly baffled by being in his arms.

Katherine couldn't help but wonder if he was playing with her, gifting her with crumbs before moving on to more substantial delicacies. She dearly hoped her admiration wasn't evident to him, especially if he felt no regard or admiration or something of the sort.

"Well, we have mutual friends, and it's only expected of me to dance with you at least once. Why, I'm sure Athelby and Aaron have both already stepped out with you, have they not?"

"Yes, they have," she grudgingly admitted, but still, that was no excuse to dance surely. Katherine shook the idea away that he actually wanted to dance with her because he liked her. Such notions helped no one, especially herself. She was a wallflower, well and truly, and no matter what her friends did to try and enable men to court her, that didn't always happen.

Who was she fooling. It never happened.

"And if you think I have forgotten the service you paid me regarding my bill at the Inn some weeks ago you're mistaken. I have not forgot that I promised I owed you for your generous service. This is merely me trying to right the wrong I placed you in that night."

Katherine couldn't meet his eye as a thought so wicked landed and flowered in her mind. The idea was tempting and at six and twenty was she brave enough to actually ask his lordship what she desired. Him, mostly. For one night at least... "While it is pleasant dancing with you, my lord, I do perhaps have something to ask, but here is not the place or time."

He pulled her close as they made a turn in the waltz. "You have me curious, Miss Martin. Please, let us talk now. Tell me what you wish."

Nerves pitted in her stomach. Could she be so bold? The words stuck in her throat, but having been privy to the affectionate nature of her friends' marriage, of their discussions of married life, it made Katherine curious. What was it like to be with a man. Did all men make a woman's toes curl in their slippers when they were kissed, like the duchess said the duke makes her? Taking a deep breath, she met his gaze with more determination than she thought possible. "Meet me on the terrace in half an hour and I shall tell you, but here is too public, too many eyes watching. Will you do that for me?"

Lord Leighton frowned, but nodded. "Of course. I shall meet you, just as you asked."

HAMISH DANCED with Lady Scottle after leaving Miss Martin with the duke and duchess of Athelby. The late Baron's wife was a beautiful woman, lush, loving and widowed, and if he played his cards right this evening, the night might end pleasurable for them both.

He stepped out of the card room, whisky in hand and watched as the woman who'd knocked him off his feet with her raw beauty an hour before slid away from her party and headed for the terrace. He didn't move, merely waited a few more minutes before he too, headed outside.

The night was warm, and there were a few couples outdoors, enjoying the balmy night air that was refreshing after being indoors with a room that smelt of wax, perfumes and human odour no one enjoyed sniffing.

Hamish strolled along the terrace, stopping to talk to those he knew, all the while sipping his whisky and looking for Miss Martin who seemed to have disappeared. He came to the end of the terrace and all that lay before him was the shadowed manicured garden.

The sound of 'psst' came from the balustrade. Looking

over he couldn't help the chuckle that escaped at seeing Miss Martin step out from a small alcove along the terrace that sat at ground level. Hamish strode down the stairs and joined Miss Martin in the secluded spot that wasn't visible to those strolling the terrace and sat on the cold stone seat.

"You're being very mysterious, and may I add a little scandalous Miss Martin. Should you be caught here with me…me especially, your reputation will be ruined."

She shook her head, dismissing his words before sitting straight and clasping her hands firmly in her lap. "You said before, you wished to help me, that you owed me after I came to your aid in Berkshire. And if you're sure your hiring of my father does not dispel your debt, then there is something I wish to ask. Before I succumb to logical thought and run away."

He chuckled, liking the fact that Miss Martin had a sense of humor. "Now I'm even more curious. Please ask, and I shall see what I can do."

"Please ensure you're sure, for once I've spoken the words there is no turning back." Her eyes were wide, and there was an edge of vulnerability to her words that he adored. He clasped his hands tight in his lap lest he reached out to touch her, any part of her, just because.

"It came to me tonight what I would like you to do for me."

"Really?" he asked, a little unsettled by the fact that he was quite alone in the garden with a woman who the more time he spent with, grew more becoming with every moment. He pulled himself up on the thought. Her father was the builder, a tradesman he'd hired to rebuild his home. He did not need to start seeing potential where there was none. Miss Martin would no sooner look at him for a husband, than he would look at her for a wife. Not that he was looking for marriage he reminded himself.

Hamish tried to remember how many drinks he'd imbibed this evening, and lost count after four. "What is it?"

She bit her bottom lip and he fought not to growl. The woman was making this bloody dreadfully hard not to kiss her.

"It is a well-known fact in my usual social sphere that I'm a wallflower. I do not delude myself with the thought of great marriage now. Did you know that I'm the oldest of all my friends? Even Cecilia, who I'm two years her senior."

His lips twitched. "I hardly believe that calls for you to be termed a matron, Miss Martin. You are still younger than myself, and I do not consider myself ancient." Although it was unfortunately and maybe even unfairly true what she was saying. By Jove, he'd even said such a thing to the duke and marquess. Not that he would admit to such things. He wasn't a complete imbecile.

"How old are you, my lord?"

"I'm six and twenty."

She half smiled, shrugging. "Then yes, we are the same age, but I fear you're forgetting what that means for a woman to what that means for a man. You're still young, perhaps even too young to even consider marriage, whereas for myself, I'm considered on the shelf and practically decrepit."

He couldn't help himself, he chuckled. "You do not look decrepit tonight, my dear." And she did not. Not at all. If anything, she was becoming one of the most beautiful and intelligent women he'd ever met. His steward couldn't speak highly enough of Miss Martin, her ideas and no-nonsense approach to tradesmen and those who worked for her father. Perhaps if she believed herself not marriageable quality he should push her toward his steward. The man wasn't attached from what he knew, and Miss Martin was from the same social set as Mr. Oakes.

Hamish went to mention such facts but held his words when he caught her eye. They were so wide, and a little conniving that he wondered and wanted to know how she wished for him to pay her back.

"Thank you for the compliment, even though I believe you hand them out like Gunther's hands out ices. Even so, this is what I propose." She took a fortifying breath and said, "I wish for you, Lord Leighton to sleep with me. Sleep with me as a man sleeps with a woman he desires, how a husband ought to sleep with his wife. How a man sleeps with his mistress."

Hamish swallowed, his body roaring to life, his mind answering yes, while his mouth seemed barren of words. He cleared his throat. "You cannot mean such things, Miss Martin. You will be ruined." Damn it, this idea was wrong. Immoral even. Miss Martin was a gently bred young lady who could still make a suitable, happy match in life. "It would not be right. I will not do it." Blast it though, the idea, now that it was in his head was not a bad one…

The image of her long legs wrapped about his hips. *Blast it.* This was not at all proper.

"I'm becoming an old maid, my lord. Let me experience what it is like for a woman to lay in the arms of a man just once. I do not want to die, whenever that shall be and wonder what I missed out on. For I'm sure after being around the duke and marquess and their wives I'm missing out on something."

He stood, needing to distance himself, although he kept himself hidden within the small alcove. Hamish understood very well what she was missing out on, and as much as his heart went out to her, this was not something he could help with. No matter how alluring the thought may be. "Our friends, should they find out would never speak to me again. They would demand that we marry, and I do not wish to marry—"

"Me?" she finished for him, hurt crossing her features before she masked the emotion.

The single word brought him up quick. "No, not you, not anyone. Not yet at least, or at all." Hamish ran a hand through his hair, his mind conjuring up all thoughts of images of what Miss Martin would look like naked on his bed, beguiling and begging for more. Her long legs, and slim waist, her dark, chocolate rich hair, laying softly against her perfect creamy shoulders.

Bloody hell…

"I will make no demands on you other than one night in your bed. Forgive me but I must speak plainly. I have a substantial dowry, more than most in my circle, but I'm passable pretty and marriage does not look forthcoming to me. I have tried to gain the attention of gentleman when they'd bothered to court me, but it has always failed and come to nothing. I will make no demands on you. My future, even if an unmarried maid, will be a future of comfort where I would not have to work if I do not wish. I merely want to experience the marriage bed and nothing more. You said you were in my debt. This would clear that debt. It is what I wish."

He came and sat beside her again, hating the fact that she damn well smelt as alluring as her words. "What if you become pregnant? What then, Miss Martin?" That would be the worst of disasters. The memory of his sister haemorrhaging, writhing in pain shot through his mind.

He looked at her, her large brown eyes wide in hope and vulnerability.

"I'm not so green that I do not know there are means, things women and men can do to stop such things. Why," she said, gesturing, "there are many mistresses in this city that are not mothers, so I know some methods are successful."

Hamish wasn't sure if he wished to strangle the woman for offering herself to him like a sacrificial lamb or damn well kiss her senseless, right here and now. His attention snapped to her lips. Damn she had a delectable mouth, lips that begged kissing, and plenty of it. How had she not been married by the gentlemen in her social set. Were they dunderheads!

"There are ways, but nothing that a well-bred young woman such as yourself should know about or even mention." And even with such ways, women still ended up pregnant. His sister for one who was very similar in frame to Katherine had been warned not to have children. The doctor termed her body as unsuitable to enable birth, something about her narrow hips, and Miss Martin's were very similar. Should she become pregnant, the thought of her dying due to his irresponsibleness was enough to turn his stomach.

She laughed, covering her mouth with her gloved hand. "I'm as old as you, Lord Leighton, not a green country miss. Have you forgotten I work at the London Relief Society with Cecilia? There is not much I have not seen or been told in some way or another. We are both adults. I'm proposing to you what I want and offering solutions to problems you're throwing at me. The way I see it is we're having a reasonable and grown up conversation. Something more women should do with the men in their lives if you must know."

No, he didn't know, and nor did he wish to be having this conversation at all. He would not sleep with a virgin simply because she did not wish to die an old maid. Why, even tomorrow a young man could bow before her at an event where they could fall madly in love, and then where would she be. Ruined.

"I will not do it. I'm sorry." He stood. "Please, since we're to work with each other on the rebuild of my home do not bring up this suggestion again. I shall repay you in any way I can, in any other way I can, but I will not take you to my bed." He would not risk her life or her honour.

Hamish swallowed when she stood, a tall woman he could almost look her straight in the eye. "Is there any way I can change your mind, my lord?"

He swallowed, fisting his hands at his side less he wrench her into his arms and kiss the hell out of her. Scare her away. Damn it all to hell. He wasn't a debaucher of virgins. And what the hell was a woman doing tempting him so? Even now, the deepening allure of her voice, her slight but determined lean toward him as she waited for a reply told him all he needed to know as to what game she played. She was playing him, but she would not win. This would not do.

"There is not. Goodnight." Hamish strode back toward the terrace steps and sought the safety of the ballroom, anything but the enticement that remained in the garden. He knew what it was to feel sorry for Adam now, but he would not bite the forbidden fruit. Not even for one night.

CHAPTER 5

Two days later, Katherine stood before Lord
Leighton's home on Berkley Square and watched as
the heavy beams were loaded off the cart and laid along
the footpath. The roof was scheduled to go on this week,
and by her calculations the home would be water tight
within three weeks. All was progressing well, and she made
a note in her diary to check that the slates for the roof were
on schedule for delivery.

"Miss Martin, how are you this afternoon?"

The familiar voice caused a shiver to run down her
spine and gathering herself, she turned and smiled in
welcome to Lord Leighton. "I'm very well, my lord. It is
fortunate that you have arrived today. As you can see," she
said, gesturing to the piles of beams, "your roof has just
arrived and looks very well indeed if I must say so myself."

Another carriage arrived on the street and the Earl
mumbled something under his breath before going to open
the door to the carriage himself when it came to a stop
before the home.

A woman in a black gown, heavy set with lace stepped

from the carriage. She was an older woman, and across the eyes was similar to his lordship. Katherine checked her gown and hoped she'd not wiped any dust across her cheek when she'd been inside looking over the construction.

Lord Leighton kissed the woman's cheek and brought her toward Katherine. "Miss Martin, may I present my mother, the dowager countess of Leighton. Mother, this is Miss Martin. Her father owns the company that is rebuilding my townhouse."

The lady's severe frown needed no explanation of exactly what she thought of Katherine and her presence on a worksite that was normally reserved for men.

"Miss Martin, singular that your father isn't present. Are you here, unchaperoned?" The slight Scottish burr went some way in explaining Lord Leighton's non-English name.

Katherine bobbed a small curtsy, holding her diary and clipboard before her breast. A means of protection perhaps, quite possibly. Lord Leighton was so very easy going, a free and happy type of man, where as his mother seemed quite severe and cross.

"My father is inside the home, your ladyship. Over-seeing the builders. We shall be on site more often over the next few weeks as we finish up this construction and make it ready for the internal decorators to begin."

"You're a woman."

Katherine raised her chin, having been subject to such conversations before, but for some reason the dowager Leighton made her being here seem more wrong that she'd ever experienced. Knowing that the woman before her was Lord Leighton's mother, did she want to impress her? Did it matter what her ladyship thought and what her opinions would make Lord Leighton think? Never before had Katherine ever responded to a man as she did with Lord

Leighton. Never before had she wanted to feel the glide of lips as much as she wished to feel his against hers.

Even so, she would not feel shame and embarrassment over her position in life. Her employment was the one source in her day where she was proud of what she achieved, for she achieved it very well.

"I am, your ladyship, but lucky for you and your son, I'm an intelligent one, just as my father is, and I can assure you once the rebuilding of your home is complete, you'll be well pleased, just as all our other clients are."

She sniffed at Katherine and looked up at the townhouse. "Oh, I so loathe having tradesmen trample through our beautiful home. I hope you have all the valuables removed, one cannot trust the men not to steal whatever is not nailed down. They are poor after all, Hamish."

Katherine bit her tongue less she cost her father a very profitable, and very connected customer. "I can vouch for our employees and state with full confidence that nothing will be damaged or stolen."

"You cannot know that for sure, why look at them," her ladyship said, her lip turning up in disdain as she watched the men unload the cart of beams. "Dirty, filthy commoners."

His lordship balked at his parent's words. "Mother, that is rude and unkind. Apologize to Miss Martin. These men are under her employment and guarantee. You cannot make such claims of them."

"I shall do whatever I wish." Her ladyship turned back toward the carriage, waiting at the door for her son to help her up the steps. "Do not forget that you're to accompany me and Lizzie to Everys' ball. We'll expect you at eight."

Katherine moved over closer to the cart, not wanting to be anywhere near Lord Leighton's mother. Never in her life had she ever met a woman with such ill manners. The carriage moved away, and the clip of his lordship's steps sounded before he came to stand beside her.

"I do apologize, Miss Martin. My mother is…well, she's stuck in her ways and there's no shifting her ideas I'm afraid."

The last of the beams was unloaded and Katherine thanked the men delivering the goods, asking them to send around their invoice as soon as they could. She turned back to Lord Leighton who stood beside her, staring at the building. "I'm here to do a job, and we shall complete the job well, on budget and in time. And I can promise you, my lord, nothing will be stolen or damaged as we do so."

"Even so, I am sorry she insinuated otherwise."

With the beams now unloaded at the building site, Katherine's day at his lordship's home was complete. Her father would take care of anything else that needed attending. Calling out her goodbye to her foreman Mr. Perry, she made her way over to her gig leaving Lord Leighton staring at his townhouse. He hurried over to her, frowning.

"You're driving yourself back to your office in London traffic?"

Katherine settled her skirts, picked up her reins and unhooked the brake. "I often drive myself about town, my lord. We have other building works happening around the city, and I cannot rely on people driving me about like some queen who cannot handle a horse."

"And you're going to another work site now, Miss Martin?"

She nodded, amused he was a little shocked by her ability. "I am. Not all of us have the luxury of lazing about all day at our clubs, or our friends' home. Some of us must work for a living, so we may pay for lords who turn up at Inns in the country and require their bills to be paid."

"Touché, I shall allow that remark, but if you think I'm

going to change my mind about what you asked of me the other night you're mistaken. I shall not change my mind, no matter how fetching you look in your drab, grey working gown."

His lordship started at his own words. Had he not meant to say such a thing? She studied him, wondering for the first time if he actually meant what he said regarding their one night of sin. "However," he continued, "I will offer a large donation in lieu of your request to the London Relief Society as recompense."

Katherine ignored the pang of hurt his words brought forth. Not that she would begrudge money to the orphanages and schools, but here was another gentleman who would offer anything other than be with her. It wasn't like she was asking for much, simply one night. She would settle for a kiss at this stage in her life, and she couldn't even gain that. She steeled her back and refused to feel sorry for herself. At least she tried to find out what married life would be like, which was better than not trying at all. "The donation would be welcome, thank you. You wish to have a working relationship and I'm quite resolved to accept your decision. But remember this Lord Leighton," she said, flicking the reins and walking on, "it does not mean I cannot ask someone else."

❦

HAMISH SAT UP IN BED, his body soaked in sweat and the bedding damp to touch. His heart beating a million times too fast in his chest. He leaned over toward the bedside cabinet and picked up the glass of water he had there, downing it quickly. After accompanying his mother and Lizzie to the Everys' ball this evening, he'd decided to stay at his mother's townhouse instead of the marquess of

Aaron's. If only to give his friends a little time away from him. He would hate to become a nuisance while he enjoyed their hospitality.

He ran a hand through his hair, his body hard, his mind awash with images of Miss Martin. Images that he knew he should not be thinking since he'd determined never to sleep with the woman, not even after her parting comment that she'd simply find someone else to do it for her. Even though the very idea of another man kissing her, touching her…. he couldn't even think it. *Bloody hell!*

He threw off the bedsheets and walked to the window, throwing up the sash and breathing in deep the cool night air. His door opened, and a slither of light flooded the room.

"Are you well, Lord Leighton? I heard the commotion in your room."

Hamish inwardly groaned. His distant cousin, Miss Lizzie Doherty was in town for the season and being fully sponsored by his parent. Worse was the fact the young girl had taken it into her head that he would make her the perfect husband.

"I'm quite well, thank you Lizzie. Please shut the door on your way out. You should not be in here."

She threw him a tentative smile, and he frowned, loathing the idea that he could be caught in the middle of the night, alone in a room with an unmarried miss. His mother would demand he marry her, and that would be disastrous for both of them. He would not be pressured into marriage, not by his mother and her desires to see him settled with someone she approved of. Marriage on such terms would only lead to heartache and resentment and would ultimately end in disaster.

"Very well. Good night, my lord."

He nodded. "Goodnight." He sighed in relief when the

door closed behind her. Whatever next! Hamish made a mental note not to stay at his mother's townhouse again, not unless Miss Doherty was back safely stowed in the country and her home or married off to a man who was at least interested in the chit.

Wanting to make sure he wasn't checked on again, Hamish locked the door and went back to bed. The dream he'd had regarding Miss Martin was an anomaly , he was sure of it. It was simply her words from the other day playing tricks in his mind. She wouldn't sleep with another man simply to throw her maidenhead out the window.

The thought of her making love with another gentleman; perhaps even enjoying the act and wishing to do it again left a pit in his gut. He wouldn't' allow it. Perhaps he should talk to her friends the duchess and marchioness to stop it. Surely, they would not condone such an absurd idea.

❧

THREE NIGHTS later Hamish stood in the Duncannon's ballroom and groaned. Damn it, the vexing Miss Martin would turn his hair grey before the season was over. She was dancing with Lord Thomas, a gentleman with a title, but little else. His pockets were well known to be for let. And the coy, fluttering eyelashes that Miss Martin kept flashing at the gentleman told Hamish exactly what he needed to know. She'd picked another man to deal with her introduction to sensual delights and was trying, right at this moment to seduce him.

He wouldn't have it, nor would he be lured in by her charm. But he would warn her of the licentious reputation of the man she danced with, hopefully sparking some sense into her.

His mother waved to him from a little way up the room, Lizzie beside her smiling in hope that he'd greet them. Unable to escape, he headed their way. "Good evening, mother, Lizzie. I did not think you were attending Duncannon's ball this evening. I thought you were for Sir Colton's musical loo."

The dowager gestured to the guests milling about them. "We're here because I wanted to see you before we quit this ball and headed over to Sir Colton's. You know Lady Colton is one of my closet friends, and she's just returned from her country estate and I so dearly wish to catch up."

"Well then," Hamish said, not wanting to postpone their departure. "Would you like me to walk you to your carriage?"

"Oh, no, we do not need assistance, Hamish, but I come with news. Your late sister's husband, Lord Russell is returning from Bath. He'll be in town for the season if you wished to see little Oscar at all."

Hamish smiled. This was good news. He always enjoyed Lord Russell's company, and adored Oscar. "I look forward to seeing them. It has been several months since we last spoke."

"I thought you would be pleased. He's staying with me at my townhouse, since he has no fixed address in London at present. You may call on him there after Friday next."

Hamish took his mother's hand and placed it on his arm. "Allow me to walk you to the carriage. You'll miss your friend if you do not leave soon."

"Oh, you're right. We must go," his mother said, allowing him to maneuverer her toward the entrance of the home.

After seeing his parent off, and Lizzie, though she begged to remain with him, Hamish strolled back into the ballroom and headed for the first footman he could see who held a tray of champagne. Taking a glass, he mingled with guests about him, promised a dance to Miss Grey, a young woman he'd often admired. The ball was a crush and standing back from the dancefloor he watched Miss Martin from afar. She was talking with Cecilia, gesturing with her hands and both of them laughing.

Miss Martin looked up and their gazes locked across the ballroom floor. A peculiar sensation thrummed through him and he took another sip of his champagne. Tonight, she was dressed in a silver muslin gown with a deep blue trim that accentuated her figure. She looked simply stunning. He didn't want to feel desire for the woman, that would never do. He did not toy with virgins, no matter how old or on the shelf they were, neither interaction was fair.

But nor did he want to miss out on sampling her sweet lips. He could imagine being the first and only man to know her intimately. To give her what she wanted. How she tempted him, more so than any other woman he'd ever known. The woman was fairly bewitching him.

Something Cecilia said caught her attention and Miss Martin looked away.

"I heard the most peculiar thing from Darcy yesterday," the duke said, coming to stand beside him but not venturing to say any more.

Hamish fought not to roll his eyes at the duke's vague disclosure, but when nothing further was stated, Hamish had to ask. "Well, are you going to tell me, or do I have to guess."

The duke chuckled and as Miss Martin was pulled out on the dancefloor for another turn about the room he ground his teeth. How much dancing could a woman do in a night. Surely, she must be getting fatigued.

He was surprised she'd not sought him out to renew her scandalous idea. The fact that she had not left a sour taste in his mouth. He adjusted his cravat, keeping his attention on anything but the woman clouding his thoughts.

Damn it all to hell.

"Very well, I shall tell you since your name was mentioned, I thought you better have your wits about you when it came to Miss Martin," the duke drawled, censure in his tone.

Hamish groaned. *They knew...*

"I already know, your grace. Miss Martin asked me for the favour after all. I have refused her of course," he added quickly when the duke's gaze turned thunderous.

His grace sighed in relief. "I am glad to hear it, although I was shocked that Miss Martin would even venture such a notion. Not that I have any say in her future or what she does, but I would not like to see her ruined since she is a particular friend to my wife."

"Are you warning me not to change my mind?" The veiled hint was not hard to miss, but the duke needn't worry, Hamish had no intention of seducing the delectable Miss Martin.

Not at all, he promised himself.

The very woman if by design crossed in front of them while dancing a reel with Sir Fraser. Her mischievous gaze met his and he scowled. Never had he ever met such a vexing woman in all his days. Was she laughing at him now? Did she suspect what they were talking about.

"By Society's standard there is no doubt Miss Martin is on the shelf, a matron in the making, even though I find her very pretty. She is from a social sphere so much beneath our own. Even so, I think it would be a mistake to trifle with her, even if she wishes. We're all friends and there will be situations in the future when we're thrown together. I do not want there to be any awkwardness or ill feelings."

"Or the fact that she could get with a child." Hamish shuddered at the thought.

The duke nodded once. "There is that as well."

Miss Martin continued to weave and dance before them, her silver gown, making her look ethereal and showcasing her long legs when the forgiving material flowed about her. Hamish swallowed. He needed to get himself together. "I promise you," he said, unable to tear his gaze away from her. "It will not be me who ruins her."

Darcy came up to them and dragged the duke out on to the dancefloor, and Hamish made his way over to Cecilia and Hunter. His reprieve was short lived when Miss Martin was brought back to her friends by her dance partner. The gentleman didn't stay long, going off and dancing again with another woman minutes later.

None of which seemed to annoy Miss Martin in the slightest, her cheeks flushed with exertion only threw images into Hamish's head he didn't need there. Of them, together, of kissing her senseless and bringing forth such a shade of pink across her cheeks and other delectable parts of her body.

There was something seriously wrong with him, and if he didn't get hold of himself soon, he'd whack himself about the ears.

KATHERINE SIPPED her ratafia and fought not to giggle, maybe there was a positive to dressing more fashionably. This ball had been quite a triumph with the amount of dance requests she'd had, and for the first time in a long time, she was enjoying herself immensely.

Poor Lord Leighton though, he did look very conflicted, and it was all her doing. And yet, she couldn't find the desire within her to stop her teasing. For the first time in her life , a wealthy, powerful lord was regarding her, his gaze all but burning admiration threatened to light her up in flames. She could get used to such inspections. A heady feeling indeed.

She had no hopes that he would take her up on her quest to lose her virginity, and nor would she look to anyone else, no matter what she told the silly man, but he did owe her, and this is what she wanted. So, if he only said the word yes, she'd meet him anywhere and at any time to spend just one night in his arms.

The thought of him above her, doing whatever it was that gentleman did above their ladies left her flustered and a peculiar flutter deep in her belly.

If she were honest with herself, she was desperate for him to kiss her. To ruin her, as scandalous as that was. Explore and take part in all the things that would normally be denied her and be damned what Society said or her friends for that matter. She would do as she wished, and deal with any consequences later if there were any.

The Marchioness and Marquess stepped out onto the ballroom floor to dance a waltz and Hamish turned to her. "Stop looking at me like that."

"Like what?" she asked, gazing at him from under her lashes, a little trick she'd seen the duchess do to the duke when she wanted to get away with something.

He leaned toward her to ensure privacy. "I will not sleep with you."

She sighed, having expected as much. "Are you sure? You do owe me, my lord, and you promised me anything that I wished. I think it very unfair you will not give me what I want." Katherine stepped closer still. "I've heard it can be quite pleasurable, my lord. Would you deny a spinster her only chance of experiencing a man in such a way?" she whispered against his ear.

She was being overly bold, but she was sick of missing out while others did not. She was forthright, opinionated and sometimes loud in her employment, and it seemed if she used similar traits in trying to gain the attentions of the opposite sex it also worked to her advantage. It certainly had this night at least.

He stilled.

"Do not play with fire, Miss Martin."

His words were low and thrummed with warning. "I hired your father's company, surely that is payment enough after your assistance at Two Toad's Inn."

She raised her brow, having not expected him to seek out that excuse. "You hired my father's company to rebuild your home because he's the best. My wishes for us are unchanged, but I will seek another if you refuse to honor your debt."

A muscle worked in his jaw and he pulled at his cravat. "The duke has warned me away from you, so you see, even if I wished to have you, I cannot."

Did he wish to have her? How delicious if he did. "The duke has nothing to do with it." Katherine cursed that Darcy had been able to swindle out of her what she desired of Lord Leighton. How the woman had accomplished such a feat, Katherine was still trying to figure out. That the duke knew of her idea was part mortifying and vexing. Did these married couples have to share everything between them?

"I will honor my debt to you, Miss Martin in any other way than this. I have already sent a donation to your charity and I will enclose the four pounds you paid for me when I settle your building fee. Please, anything but what you ask."

He ran a hand through his hair, his words torn and with a pleading edge to them. Her insecurities threatened. Was she so horrid, so tall and thin that he was worried she would not inspire him enough when they were alone for him to lay with her? Of course, she was, and she was a fool to hope otherwise.

Katherine swallowed the lump that formed in her throat at the mortifying thought. She would put a stop to the duchess and marchioness giving her beautiful gowns to wear, having their maids do up her hair in fashionable, intricate styles. The false bravado they were giving her was giving her airs that she did not need, nor what others saw. She was at her core, still the plain, lanky woman from trade who was only here due to who she knew, not because of what she was.

Shame washed through her and she blinked, horrified that tears threatened to spill over her cheeks. "Lord Leighton your words have made me realize what a terrible and shameful thing I've been asking you. Please forgive me and know that I shall not ask again, nor will I state your debt as unpaid. I never sought repayment in any case, it is not in my nature to do so. I think these past months have made me see what I shall never have, and I saw an opportunity to gain it and in doing so I've embarrassed both you and myself. I'm so very sorry."

Katherine managed a quick curtsy before she walked from the room, needing to get away from everyone less they see her upset. She would return home and send a missive apologizing to her friends for leaving early. Better that than to make a spectacle of herself in public.

THE FOLLOWING MORNING Katherine walked out of the breakfast room, having come down early after a restless night. It suited her plans in any case as she had to oversee more of the roof construction at Lord Leighton's townhouse.

"You're not wearing those, I hope," Jane said, all but floating down the staircase in a light blue muslin gown, her blonde hair perfect and coiled to perfection. The vision of her cousin only amplified her own shortcomings and she snatched up her riding gloves from the small table beside the front door. Gentleman wanted women who were beautiful and full figured, they did not care for wit or intelligence, such as she possessed.

"As you see. I often wear breeches and father is aware of the fact." Katherine placed the grey felt cap on her head which all but covered her hair, and glancing in the looking mirror, she would easily pass as a man. Certainly, her figure was not the most feminine and not desired at all by Lord Leighton. He'd certainly made that plain enough last night, and she had been dressed as well as any woman there.

"I suppose with your long legs and body that doesn't have one ounce of womanly curves, you'll pass as a gentleman easily enough."

Katherine stopped at the front door, debating whether she'll let her vexing relative get away with such an insult or simply ignore it. She chose to ignore it, and pulling the door open, strolled from her home.

The day was young, the air fresh and crisp and hailing a hackney cab, she headed over to Mayfair. Their workers would have arrived by now, and just as she presumed, upon arrival she was happy to see the men busy up on the roof.

"Can I help you?" A man asked when she walked through the front doors and into the entrance hall of the home.

Katherine stifled a scream, having not seen the gentleman standing by the library doors.

"Lord Leighton, you frightened me. I did not see you standing there," she said, coming over to him.

His eyes widened, his attention snapping to her legs. "You're in breeches."

It wasn't a question and Katherine raised her brow. "As you see. I often wear breeches in such a way for this employment, it enables me to move about more freely and help the men here when required. It also saves my gowns from being unnecessarily ruined."

His lordship swallowed, but didn't reply straight away, just continued to stare. "You cannot," he said, regaining his voice at last, "go upstairs, with a group of men in those breeches."

Katherine turned on her heel and headed for the staircase. "Oh, don't worry, my lord. The men are quite used to seeing me dressed like this. As for you, I do apologize for startling you so, but I assure you, once I have completed my inspection here I shall leave you to yourself, where there will be no chance of me embarrassing you."

❦

HAMISH TOOK a calming breath as he watched Miss Martin climb the stairs, the men's breeches showcasing every long, sculptured line of her legs, her small buttocks that were only minimally covered by her bottle green jacket.

He'd never seen a woman dressed in such attire, and as ridiculous as it would seem, he damn well liked it. More women should wear such clothing if they looked as well in it as Miss Martin.

He followed her up the stairs, unable to tear his gaze away from her ass. She never turned to look back at him or engage him in further conversation. He stewed, worried that their conversation last night had insulted her in some way.

Who was he deluding, of course she'd been hurt. He hadn't missed her tears after his denial of her. But what Miss Martin didn't know was his denial of her was not because he did not want to have her, run his hand along every line of her body, find out if she was as smooth and sweet as he imagined, but because his want of her went against his better judgement. He may be one of the rogues of London, but even he had rules.

They had a working relationship and that is where it would end. Should they sleep together and she fell pregnant, he would be honor bound to marry her, a situation that he did not look for in his future. And then for Miss Martin to thicken with child, the idea made him break out in a cold sweat and his heart trembled.

His sister May's atrocious labour with her son was something he never wanted to see again. May, like Miss Martin was delicate and small boned. Neither of them even looked suitable to having children. The doctor who'd looked after his sister had even stated that women who were small across the hips, delicate boned and thin were not suited to go through the trauma of birthing a child.

Miss Martin might go on to marry and have children, take such a risk, but it would not be by him.

They made the first floor landing and headed toward the ballroom which was a hive of activity. Hamish could see the foreman in conversation with two of his workers, all of them looking up at the beams going up in the new roof.

The room, with the structure coming together was starting to take shape into what it had once been, except for the newly designed balcony that opened to allow guests to congregate outdoors, even if up on the first floor of the home.

"Do you like the design, my lord?" Miss Martin asked, coming to stand beside him out on the balcony that looked over his large, manicured back garden.

The air smelt of oak and some of the workers had set up saws on the newly constructed balcony and used it to cut wood to suit their needs. Hamish walked out to where the balustrade was taking shape. A stonemason had been brought in to create one that matched the terrace below, and large stone pillars were already beneath them taking some of the weight the new structure placed on the home.

"I trust it'll not collapse," he said half joking. It was a very long way down after all.

"Most certainly it will not. We've built support beams into the home itself that run beneath the ballroom floor. As you know, most of it was damaged, and has been replaced. Before we did that, and because you stipulated you wished to have a balcony terrace, we laid the support beams. Of course, the balcony is also supported from beneath, but once the stone pillars are in, this balcony is not going anywhere."

"Is it safe for us now?" he asked, not quite convinced of her words yet.

"Yes, for the few of us who're on it. Obviously, you're not holding a ball where as many as twenty people could be standing out here at any one time. Until the pillars are finished I wouldn't suggest such a thing, but just us and the couple of workers at a time is perfectly safe."

Hamish nodded and glanced back through the terrace doors, those too were new and still in their natural form, not painted or with any handles. "You've done a marvellous job so far. Give my thanks to your father."

She smiled, and pride filled her face, making her look even prettier than he thought possible. And he'd turned her down. Refused her one wish...

"Thank you, Lord Leighton. Father will be pleased to hear you say so."

"I'm not blind to your own input and hard work on my home, and I do thank you too. I will recommend your company to anybody I know who's looking for a master craftsman."

She started to walk off and he followed.

"We're only doing our job, and soon enough we'll be out of your way and your life can return to normal."

Normal...boring. He enjoyed having her here, talking about things other than gossip or the latest fashions. Miss Martin was an interesting woman, a very smart and educated one at that. "Are you heading somewhere else?" he asked, as she waved goodbye to the foreman and continued toward the staircase. Maybe they could extend this tête-à-tête with a impromptu lunch.

"I am. I have to inspect a building out at Richmond we've just finished building. We build homes as well as repair them you see. Always busy."

Hamish caught her hand and pulled her to a stop as she made the footpath. It wasn't until Miss Martin pulled her hand away that he realized he still held it. "Miss Martin, will you do the honor of allowing me to call you by your first name? Calling each other Miss and Lord seems overly formal, and we're friends are we not? If you feel more comfortable only calling me by my given name when we're here or alone that would work too."

She met his gaze, a small teasing grin lifting her lips.

"Alone, Lord Leighton, you didn't wish to be alone with me, so perhaps it's best we stay formal and aloof."

"And if I said I do not wish to remain formal and aloof." Why he suggested it Hamish couldn't fathom, nor did he regret his words, which was something that he couldn't fathom either.

Miss Martin climbed up in her carriage and leaned a little out the window. She contemplated him for a moment, a small frown line marring her usually perfect brow. "My name is Katherine, but Kat to my friends. You may call me either one, in private or public, in either locale does not bother me."

Katherine. He liked her name, and the shortened version Kat had a vixen ring to it. It suited her. He picked up her hand that lay atop the carriage door and kissed it. "Until we meet again, Katherine," he said, liking the fact that her cheeks coloured with the lightest shade of rose.

"You didn't tell me your name, Lord Leighton?" she said, grinning.

"You can call me Hamish." He stepped back and watched as the carriage pulled away and made its way around Berkley Square. *Kat...*His gut clenched at what such a name brought forth in his imagination and he couldn't help but wonder if she'd be like a wildcat, untamed and feral or sweet and affectionate. Or perhaps she was both, and that thought brought a flush to his own body.

He shouldn't want her like he did, but there was something infinitely different about her. Perhaps it was the fierce independence and self-assurance that attracted him so. When in his Society he had seen moments of her where she'd looked fearful, but walking within the *ton's* viper nest that was to be expected. Hamish turned and started back toward the house, his man of business had asked him to go through some letters he'd left in his library, and deal with the business of two of his country estates. Normally he would shirk most of this work off to his steward, but not today. Katherine's unwavering dedication to her employment made his own lacklustre approach shameful. He ought to do better for his tenants and those who worked for him.

He ought to spend less time socializing and more time looking after the things that actually mattered. Since seeing Katherine again, he had to admit that his bad luck had waned, in fact, had disappeared.

Miss Martin, was out making a difference in the world and so too would he. A self-deprecating laugh escaped. She was already a good influence on him and his pampered ways.

CHAPTER 6

The duchess hosted an afternoon tea party for some of the upper echelons of the *ton* two days after Katherine's run in with Lord Leighton, and unfortunately, or fortunately depending on Katherine's disposition on any given day, she was invited.

The never-ending tittle-tattle of gossip, of gowns and who was recently returned to town and those that had scuttled back to their country estates was all that she'd heard, nodded to and gasped at the past two hours. If she did not escape soon she'd simply expire of boredom.

Excusing herself from three recently married women who were fixated on finding the proper children's nurse for their impending children, Katherine moved away and started toward Cecilia who looked as bored as she did.

Upon joining Cecilia, the lady Cecilia was talking to made her excuses and moved away, thankfully leaving them alone. "Save me, or I shall tell you everything I know about nannies, for I have just had a very lengthy and involved discussion on the topic."

Cecilia chuckled, handing her a plate with a sugar biscuit on it. "Eat one of these, it'll make you feel better."

Katherine took a bite, and almost choked when Lord Leighton's mother entered the room with her young charge whom she was sponsoring this year. The woman looked almost friendly when she greeted the duchess and looking about the room she nodded and waved to women she knew, but her ladyship's ease and enjoyment slipped somewhat when she spotted Katherine.

Instead of simply moving her gaze along and joining in with her friends' conversations, she came over to them instead, her visage one of displeasure and ire.

"Lady Aaron, so lovely to see you again and I must thank you for housing my son for the next few weeks after the dreadful fire. You're the best of people to open your home so."

Cecilia dropped a curtsy and Katherine quickly followed, having forgotten to show her respect to the matriarch of Society. "Lord Leighton is always welcome, as well you know. It is a pleasure to have him as a guest." Cecilia turned to Katherine.

"Lady Leighton, may I present my friend, Miss Katherine Martin. She is a good friend of mine and the duchess of Athelby and is a founding member of the London Relief Society that I run."

Katherine bobbed a quick curtsy again, and then remembered she'd already done so. Heat spread across her cheeks and she took a calming breath. What did it matter if her ladyship was glaring at her, her displeasure obvious to any who looked their way. The woman was nothing to her, only the mother of the man whose face kept her up at night. Awake with a longing she didn't understand, but desperately wanted to know.

"Lady Leighton and I have already met, although it was very brief."

The woman's eyes narrowed, but she feigned surprise. "Oh, of course, at my son's home. You are the builder's daughter are you not?" She smiled to temper her barb. "How is the family business going my dear? From seeing your harried appearance, the other day, I can only assume that you have little time for frivolities like outings such as these. You looked quite tired if I must say so myself. Perhaps in future you will consider your health and whether attending such events as these would be in your best interests."

Katherine swallowed the heated retort that formed on her tongue, and instead bit into her little cake, all but halting any thoughts of replying.

Not that she had to worry about such things, as Cecilia wound her arm within hers and lifted her chin. "Did you know, Lady Leighton that Katherine and I grew up together, in Cheapside. We were neighbors from a very early age. As you're aware, my father is a barrister."

Lady Leighton's appearance did not change, but the warmth in her eyes for Cecilia diminished a little. "I did not know that, Lady Aaron. How interesting."

"Isn't it," Cecilia said, smiling quickly at Katherine. "But enough about us, tell us about the young woman you've brought today. She seems very sweet."

To her credit, Lady Leighton took the opportunity to change the subject away from Cecilia and Katherine's upbringing in trade. "She is my niece, Lizzie Doherty. I'm sponsoring her this season and hoping to have her married and settled by next season. Our family is in need of an uplifting event, such as a wedding."

"Are there any suitors that have made their intention

known, your ladyship," Katherine asked, simply not to be standing beside them like a mute.

"There have been a couple, but she's refused their offers. I do believe she holds fond feelings for my son, Hamish, and what a good match they would make, but alas, he does not seem to return her feelings and so she's quite downcast."

"But they are cousins. Is marriage between them even desired?" Katherine blurted before she thought better of it.

Her ladyship's eyes widened, and her mouth worked but no words came out for a few moments. Katherine inwardly cursed for asking, for her ladyship did not appreciate her question.

"Let me assure you, Miss Martin, cousins have married and are allowed to marry, so your question that reeked of disgust can be kept to yourself, if you don't mind. Hamish would be lucky to marry such a lady, for that is what Miss Lizzie Doherty is, unlike some of those who walk among us."

Cecilia gasped, and Katherine studied her ladyship a moment, what she found there was very lacking indeed. She was born to privilege, was a Countess, but she was unkind and that's all she had to be for Katherine to take her measure. "Do you mean me, your ladyship?"

The woman glanced at her with disdain. "How dare you ask me such a thing? I would never be so rude."

"I beg to differ," Katherine said, placing down her now empty plate on a small table beside them. She turned toward her friend. "I must go, Cecilia darling, but we're still on for De Vere's ball Friday?"

"You needn't leave, Katherine. Come ladies, let us not quarrel."

Katherine threw one more scathing glance at Lady Leighton and walked from the room. Conversation swam about her, and thankfully those in attendance hadn't seemed to notice that she'd disagreed with the countess. But what a disagreeable woman she was. So high and mighty and thinking she was not worthy of having friends in this sphere of Society.

And perhaps she was not, she was a builder's daughter after all, but by happenstance and simple luck she'd become friends with a duchess and her best friend had married a marquess and so like it or not, she now had a foot in both levels of Society.

A waiting footman handed her cloak and called a hackney cab for her. Katherine sighed, laying her head back against the squabs. Lady Leighton was an unpleasant harridan. But why did she dislike her so much? It is not as if she knew her, would've heard any rumors as there weren't any. Katherine wasn't a woman who courted scandal, and if she removed the one time she'd asked Lord Leighton to sleep with her, she'd done nothing at all.

She thought back to when she'd met her ladyship at the building site. Was there something she saw in Lord Leighton's eyes that had worried her. Had she sensed her son was attracted to Katherine, and attraction that all but hummed between them whenever they were near?

Katherine certainly did, and that very allure had been the reason she'd asked him to lie with her. Even if he was adamant he wouldn't grant her wish, it could not stop her from dreaming about being with him so. She'd seen often enough the glances and small affection touches Darcy and Cecilia made and received in turn. Over the time she'd been friends with them, seeing them married and happy left an ache in her chest. If she could not find a gentleman to marry, not to say she hadn't tried, for she had, for years, she at least wanted to know the touch of a man, to know if she were missing out and ought to look again.

The carriage rolled to a stop before her home and thanking the footman who raced down the house's stairs to open the carriage door, she went inside, only to come to a halt in the hall at the sight of Jane, standing before Lord Leighton, a blushing, gushing mess.

"Dearest Katherine, look who has paid us a call. You know Lord Leighton of course."

Katherine had just about had enough of spiteful women and seeing Jane all flustered and preening over Lord Leighton in her home left her teeth to ache. Katherine ripped off her gloves and unpinned her hat, handing them to a waiting footman before turning to face them both.

"Good afternoon, my lord. Can I help you with anything?"

Jane chuckled. "You must forgive my cousin, my lord. It seems her social niceties were lost along with her youth." The brazen little hussy reached up and plucked an invisible piece of lint from his lordship's jacket, and Lord Leighton stepped away, uncertainty clouding his eyes.

"On the contrary, Miss Digby. I have never known Miss Martin to be other than a pillar of manners and kindness. Something that you may wish to aspire to."

Jane paled at being chastised and Katherine fought not to crow at his kindness toward her.

"I was hoping to have a private word with you, Miss Martin. If you're free," he asked, catching her gaze.

"I suppose you shall not need a chaperone since you're well past that necessity," Jane said, clearly out to make her point now that Lord Leighton had told her off. "Although, you really ought to start wearing a cap, dearest cousin, it would cause less scandal if you're to attend gentleman callers in private."

"Thank you, Jane, you may go," she said, her words

blunt and to the point. Katherine moved past her with little regard, having had enough of people judging her simply because she didn't fit into their mould of what they expected women to be.

Lord Leighton followed her into the library and she gestured him to take a seat before the fire that was alight, ready for her father when he would return home later in the day. Katherine sat beside him and tried to shake off her annoyance and damn it, the hurt her cousin caused by her words.

"How can I help you, Lord Leighton?" she asked, settling her skirts about her legs.

He was quiet for a moment, fiddled with his cravat before he seemed to gather himself. "I wanted to discuss what you asked of me."

Katherine inwardly groaned, not wanting nor in the mood to discuss such matters. Not today at least. After her run in with his mother at the duchess of Athelby's afternoon tea and now her cousin, her disposition to remain nice after hearing why he couldn't sleep with her waned.

"There is no need to explain anything, my lord. I understand perfectly well."

"Do you?" he asked, watching her intensely.

What did he see when he looked at her, beauty, desperation, she was certainly the latter, but the former she'd never claimed to be. Passable was what she heard one gentleman state, rich but not biddable another, too much work if one was willing to take her on.

"You've already explained your reasons, my lord. You do not need to do so again." She went to stand, and he clasped her hand, pulling her back down.

"I wasn't entirely truthful when we spoke last. I used the excuse of rank, of our mutual friends and their reactions should our interlude become known, especially when

I'd promised never to darken your bedroom's door. I used your potential fall from grace, the ruination of your reputation should you get with child."

Her heart squeezed at the recitation. Katherine pulled her hand away, folding them into her lap. "I think they are worthy enough excuses, you do not need to come up with any more."

"I do, because I fear you think it's because I do not desire you."

Heat rose on Katherines cheeks and she bit her lip, unsure as to what to say to such honesty. "Then what is it?" she asked, unable to stop herself.

"I know you have not asked for anything but one night in my bed, but I wonder if you've thought of the consequences of such actions. I do not hide from the fact that I have had lovers, many of them but they are seasoned lovers, players of this game and they know how to play the game without consequences. If you understand what I'm saying."

She understood perfectly well. "You mean children, and that our one night may result in me carrying your child. Something you do not wish for any more than I, my lord." Not that the idea of having Lord Leighton's child didn't make her weak at the knees. Whoever persuaded him into marriage, into love would be very well pleased. Under his charm and beauty, he was kind, not vicious. Was there not a saying that rakes made the best husbands...

"I've seen you around the duchess and marchioness. I've seen your wistful looks at their happiness. If we were to be together, I fear you'll want more of me than I'm willing to commit. And that is no reflection on you," he said, reaching out to clasp her hand. "It's me. I do not wish for marriage, not now at least and perhaps never."

His thumb glided over the top of her hand and

Katherine realized he still had hold of her. "Do not think for one moment Katherine that I do not desire you. From the very first moment we met I've had a peculiar craving to kiss you. To speak plainly, the hunger you rouse in me isn't something I'm familiar with and I do not trust myself with you. And that, can lead to folly and consequences," he declared his voice thick with emotion.

She met his gaze and a shiver stole over her. "I'm not asking for marriage or children. Nor will I hide from life. I refuse to do so any longer. I wish to experience everything I can before I die, and while I understand your fears, it does not mean I cannot seek out what I want to know. What I want to feel."

ॐ

HAMISH STARED at Katherine as her declaration brought a flush to her cheeks and a sparkle in her dark brown eyes. Were his fears unreasonable? Perhaps, but it did not change the fact that women died during childbirth, thin, delicate women like Miss Martin. Never before in his life had he been asked for a night of sin with a woman of respectable standing. His liaisons had always been over before they started, he'd never tried to deepen connections, grow to care for the women he bedded. It was not what he wanted.

"My coming here was to explain my reasons behind denying you. I did not want you imagining anything other than what I've stated here this evening."

"Thank you for being so honest with me and because you have, I shall be in return."

"Really," he said, curious. "Do tell me."

Katherine chuckled, pulling him back toward the chaise lounge to sit. "I had believed you turned me down because I'm not what you find attractive. I've seen you at balls and parties too, the curvy, bountiful women with blonde golden locks that you seek out." She gestured toward herself. "I'm obviously none of those things. So, in an odd way, it's a relief to know your reasons."

⊗⊛⊗

HIS GAZE SLID over her form, from her face down to her toes, and heat spiralled in her stomach. She bit her lip, wanting him with a desperation that she'd never felt before. It was the oddest thing, and yet she could not help herself. Was it because he'd denied her that she wanted him so, or simply because he was the only man who'd ever brought the feelings that were rioting inside of her to life.

"But now you know the reasons behind my choice, do not think it's because I do not find you attractive. Why even now all I can think about is what you want from me. What I'd love to do to you."

Katherine gasped, unable to help it. What he'd love to do to her? What did that even mean? Her heart thumped hard in her chest and her light muslin gown felt tight about the breasts. What was he doing to her? Raw hunger crossed his features and she shivered.

"Damn it," he growled, moving quickly and taking her lips in a searing kiss, his hands against her jaw tipped up her chin so he could deepen the embrace.

The world spiralled out of control and one word went around and around in her head. *Yes...*

So, this is what made her friends all dreamy eyed when talking of their husbands... Hamish moaned when she mimicked what he was doing with his tongue and a beautiful ache thrummed between her legs. She squirmed, needing to be closer to him. He pulled her hard against his chest, the thump of her heart loud in her ears.

Katherine kissed him back with eagerness, willingness to know more, to experience this side of life. She'd never been kissed before and being kissed now by a veritable rogue of the *ton*, a man who was famous for his beautiful women and quick liaisons made her even more desperate to do as much as he'd allow.

For there was no doubt that this wicked embrace he was bestowing on her was simply a chink in his armor. She was going to kiss him until he stopped and be damned what happened after the event.

Her breasts raked across his chest as she wrapped her arms about his neck. His kiss was ardent, deep and claiming. The glide of his hand on her thigh made her shiver, and it was only when the cool air kissed her ankles that she wondered at his loss of control. Had he changed his mind? Was he willing to sleep with her now that he'd kissed her?

Oh, please say that you are.

Hamish wrenched out of her arms, setting her back to her side of the chaise and rose, running a hand through his hair and leaving it on end. "God's blood." He took a couple of steps back, colliding with the chair behind him and almost falling over. Righting himself, he watched her, his eyes wide, his lips reddened by their activity.

She'd done that. She'd rattled one of the most sought-after gentleman in the *ton*. It was a heady feeling and she stood, wanting more of the same.

He held out his hand to halt her steps. "No. We cannot. I cannot. I'm sorry," he said, bolting out of the room like a startled horse.

Katherine watched the empty doorway until she heard the front door slam closed behind him. She flopped down on the leather wingback chair, finally, after six and twenty years she'd had her first kiss. And not a chaste, peck on the lips, but a true, toe curling, heart pounding kiss. One that made everything else pale in comparison. If being in Lord Leighton's arms was as enjoyable as she'd just experienced, there was no wonder women married men or indulged in scandalous affairs.

Who would not want that every day?

And now all she had to do was figure out how to get him to kiss her again. She stared at the flames licking the wood in the hearth. There was the Curzon ball coming up that she was to attend with Darcy and Cecilia. Maybe she would put off her idea of wearing one of her own gowns and borrow one from Darcy instead. Darcy had loved nothing more than to shock the *ton* of their sensibilities prior to marrying the Duke of Athelby, and that's exactly what Katherine needed to do with Lord Leighton. Seduce him in to having her or at the very least, kissing her again. Either option would be enjoyable.

CHAPTER 7

Hamish arrived late to the Curzons' ball and there was a very special reason for doing so. He wasn't normally a coward, didn't shy away from events that could prove trying, but tonight he wasn't so sure he was up for battle.

This would be a very particular battle with the very charming, very good at kissing, Miss Martin. It had been four days since he'd kissed her in her library, an event that should never have happened. He'd no sooner told her why he wouldn't sleep with her, to then maul her on the settee.

One touch of her soft lips, the soft little gasps as he took her mouth with his, made him hard. He greeted his hostesses, stopping to chat with them for a time, though his mind was elsewhere. Was she still here? It was after midnight, and their group of friends often attended more than one event when out in Society.

"Lord Leighton."

He heard his name and inwardly swore when he recognized the voice. His cousin Lizzie Doherty waved and walked toward him. Excusing himself from Lord Curzon he met her, away from prying ears as one never knew what was going to come out of the chits mouth at any one time.

"Lizzie, how lovely you look this evening."

She dipped into a quick curtsy, grinning up at him. He tempered his annoyance, the young woman was sweet, if a little naïve and annoying at times. She was still family and he would not be short with her, no matter how much he longed to seek out Miss Martin if only to apologize for his ungentlemanly behaviour the other day.

"Thank you, cousin, that is very kind of you. Your mama said that blue was your favourite color and so I thought this would please you most especially."

Hamish made a mental note to tell his mother to mind her own business in future. "Did she, well, the color suits you very well."

She took his arm, and although forward, Hamish used the opportunity to deliver her to his mother whom he spied over near the supper room doors. Her pleased expression at seeing him with Lizzie warned Hamish, and he knew exactly what she was about.

His parent beamed, leaning up to kiss his cheek as he came to stand before her. With well-practised expertise he extracted Lizzie's arm without causing offence.

"You're very late, Hamish. We've been waiting for you to arrive, you owe your cousin a dance before we take our leave."

He inwardly groaned while nodding in agreement. "Of course, I'll dance with my cousin. When there is another set I shall come and collect you."

"There is to be a waltz next, just before supper. I think now is as good a time as any."

Hamish held out his arm to his cousin, and she all but bounced while taking it. Leading her onto the floor a flash of red caught his eye and looking he stumbled as he recognized Miss Martin, settling into the arms of Lord Lacelles, an Earl of impeccable character and unlimited funds. He could marry whomever he pleased, whenever he pleased being the only child and without family after the death of his parents at an early age.

If the content grin and sparkling eyes that she all but batted toward the Earl were any indication, Miss Martin was well pleased.

"Shall we, Lord Leighton?" his cousin asked.

Hamish wrenched his gaze from Miss Martin, and instead pulled Lizzie into his. He allowed the flow of the music to soothe his ire, but it was dastardly hard when Miss Martin kept floating by, the sound of her joyful laughter like a punch to the gut.

He didn't say a lot to Lizzie for fear of being sharp, but somehow he managed one or two questions, although he could not for the life of him recall if she even answered or what those answers were. As soon as the dance was over, he marched her back to his mother, settled them at the supper room table and left to seek out his friends where most decidedly Miss Martin would be.

Their table was full when he came over to them, the Earl of Lacelles sitting with them where he would normally reside. The duke stood as he came up to them, smiling in welcome.

"Leighton, let me have a chair fetched for you," he said, calling over a footman to attend him.

Soon enough Hamish was seated alongside them all, and yet the annoyance that flowed through his veins would not abate. He'd hoped to speak to Katherine alone, but the likelihood of that at present seemed slim. Darcy, Cecilia and Miss Martin sat at the table, eating lobster patties and drinking wine. They were laughing and chuckling about all kinds of things that eluded him.

And what baffled him when he didn't wish it to, was Miss Martin avoiding any sort of eye contact with him. When he'd spoken she'd simply turned to the Earl of Lacelles beside her and chatted quietly. When he commented on topics their friends raised she busied herself with her meal or wine.

What game was she playing….?

The good conversation flowed, and determined to have her look at him, Hamish simply waited, stared at her and sought patience.

The moment she did it was like a physical blow to his gut. In her dark orbs, there was no masking the burning desire for him. Where had she learnt such a thing? A woman he was certain had never been kissed before his slip the other day. But she had learned the art of flirting, and his body reacted accordingly.

The duke cleared his throat, and Hamish looked to his friend seated to his left, the duke's raised brow told Hamish he'd seen their silent communication.

"I hope you know what you're doing, Hamish. I do not want to see Miss Martin hurt under any circumstances. She does not have a brother to fight for her honor, so be mindful of it."

Hamish took a long pull of his wine. "I do not intend to hurt her, and nothing will occur in any case. I've told her I shall not do what she asks and that's the end of it."

"Really," the duke scoffed. "That look that just passed between the two of you already tells me something has occurred."

He refused to squirm under the duke's commanding presence or knowing eyes. Hamish lowered his voice. "I kissed her, that is all and all it ever will be."

The guests started to make their way to the ballroom, and Hamish stood, not wanting to continue his current conversation. To prove his point, he walked from the supper room and sought out Lady Grey, a widow and a woman whom he was very fond of, a woman who'd more than once warmed his bed. He needed a distraction, a reminder that Miss Martin wasn't anyone special. She was simply a mutual friend he'd kissed.

A footman passed with a silver tray full of champagne glasses and he swiped one and drank it down placing it back on the tray before the footman had gone two steps. Lady Grey threw him an amused glance as he bowed before her, before taking her hand and all but dragging her onto the dance floor.

He moved with her through the intricate steps of the reel, reminding himself that she was the type of woman he enjoyed taking to his bed. She was a woman of medium height, with rich golden blonde locks that accentuated her striking face and equally striking bosom. Her rounded figure and hips that had a little flesh on them, were just enough to hold on to when riding a wave of pleasure. And she was well versed in avoiding consequences that such bed sport often produced.

"I hope I'm being helpful in distracting you Lord Leighton from whatever vexes you so."

He looked down at her, surprised by such a question. "How do you mean?"

She laughed, a sultry, condemning sound that went straight to his conscience. "Who is she?" she asked, meeting his gaze, her features serious of a sudden.

He twirled her, before moving down the line of dancers. "No one." The lie tasted bitter on his tongue and glanced up to see Katherine watching him, her attention on him but a second before moving onto his dance partner then away.

If he wished to see hurt on her features, he was disappointed. No such reaction occurred, merely boredom and curiosity. Did she not care? Did she truly only wish for him to take her to his bed, one night and then they would part. Was he being too emotional over the whole concept, when she was looking at it as merely an enlightening experience she would enjoy before moving on into spinsterhood well and truly.

"She's very pretty, not beautiful, but passable."

Passable? The word sent his ire to soar. Katherine was more than passable. Damn it, she was growing to be one of the most beautiful women of his acquaintance. The women he usually dallied his days away with were nothing but painted up doxy's. Their fortune the only difference between them and the Convent Garden whores.

Shame washed over him at the thought. It was men like him that enabled such sport against walls in alleyways, in rowdy houses of ill repute. It was men like him who slept with women, where the slightest interest was sometimes enough for one to lift a gown in a vacant room at a ball, or deserted passageway. If the women of his acquaintance were whores, then so too was he.

"She is lovely, but she is not up for conversation. Nor should I be dancing with you simply to spite her."

Lady Grey grinned up at him, mischief in her eyes. "Is that what I am right now? Am I a woman to cause jealousy in another simply so you can gain what you want?"

If only it was as simple. There was no doubt he wanted Katherine, but it was she who sought him out, wanted him just as much. A heady, alluring concept he'd never experienced before in his life.

Thankfully the dance came to an end, and returning Lady Grey to her friends, Hamish made a hasty exit and started toward Miss Martin. She watched his approach, the lift of one brow, challenging and vexing at the same time, made his desire for her twofold.

He walked past her, clasping her hand and pulling her around to follow him. She did without a word, and they exited into a passageway that led into a conservatory. The room smelt as exotic plants and fruits. Without waiting, and with no words spoken between them, he pushed her up against the wall beside the door and took her mouth in a searing, punishing kiss.

She moaned the instant their lips met, her hands wrapping about his neck and holding him close. Hamish pinned her there, wanting to keep her just as she was forever. His mind was a cluster of unfathomable, confused thoughts, of what was right and wrong. What he wanted to do versus what he should do.

The feel of her hand sliding down his back, coming to rest on his rump sent heat to his cock and he hardened further. And damn it, he was so hard already it physically hurt.

He kissed his way down her neck, the scent of apples that sprung from her gown intoxicating him. He clasped her bottom, holding her against him and rocked, reveled in her gasp of surprise, before that little gasp turned into a siren's call and she undulated against him, seeking her own pleasure.

Hamish was certain she didn't know what she sought, but the body, when aroused didn't need past experiences to know what it craved. Here, at the Curzons' ball wasn't the place for them, and he would not deflower her here amongst the *ton*, but he would have her.

That he had no doubt of, not any longer. When they were apart he thought of little else, other than to be with her again, even if simply to talk. And when near her, the urge to be tactile, take her gloved hand and dance, was overwhelming. He would no longer deny either of them what they wanted.

"We cannot here, Katherine." His words were breathless, his heart pumping loud in his ears.

"Where then?" she asked, meeting his gaze. "Surely we can come together sometime soon. It is for only one night after all." She glided her thumb across his lips and he playfully bit it.

"Sometime soon, I promise, but not here, not now. I will not be such a blaggard and take you in a conservatory up against a wall."

"And yet," she said, a playful tilt to her head. "The thought of such a way has me curious. Is it even possible?"

Oh, dear god. He hardened further at the image that roused in his mind. "It's possible, believe me, a lot is possible when one wants it enough."

A small frown formed between her perfect brows. "You'll think me silly, but how is it possible. We both need to stand and so I thought…"

Hamish reached down, and hoisted her gown up, lifting her legs at the same time and wrapping them about his hips. Instinctively she wrapped her arms about his neck, her eyes wide with surprise and enlightenment.

It was the worst mistake of his life, for having her like this, his cock hard up against her heat almost doubled him over with need. "Do you understand now?" he rasped, unable to help but to rub himself against her core.

She all but thrummed in his arms, helping him with his undulation. "Don't move, Katherine." He kissed her hard and the little minx moved again. He moaned, but somewhere in the lustful recess of his mind, he set her on her feet, quickly righting her gown before stepping back fighting to control his emotions.

"You should return to the ball before you're missed. Go

back through the main entrance hall, the guests will simply think you've returned from the retiring room."

Hamish didn't move, needing to stay exactly where he was lest he drag her down onto the marble bench and take her here and now, and bedamned who caught them.

Katherine, her eyes cloudy with unsated need, a feeling he was well and truly feeling himself right at the moment, stood before him, leaning close before kissing him softly. She met his gaze as she stopped the chaste embrace, holding his gaze.

"I'll await your summons, Lord Leighton."

His gut tightened at the thought of having her beneath him. Without distractions or the possibility of interruption. "Hamish, please," he reminded her.

She turned and headed for the door, stopping to glance over her shoulder. "Don't take too long, Hamish. After what you showed me tonight, I may seek you out if you do."

Body roaring with need, he grabbed hold of the small cabinet beside him and didn't let go until she was out of sight. When he'd pulled her away from the ball he'd not planned to engage in such antics.

All lies when he cared to admit it to himself. He'd been so distracted seeing her dancing with someone else, that all his thoughts had centered on claiming her, letting her know in uncertain terms that it was he who would deflower her, not some other man.

Blast it all to hell. What was he going to do? After tasting her, having her sweet, willing body hard up against his, tempting him like sin, there was no way in hell he wasn't going to give her what she wanted. But then what? One night only in her arms?

Something told him that would never do. To fully gauge and experience all that could be between them they should at least have two. He would put the proposition to her when he saw her next, which would be sooner rather than later.

THE CARRIAGE RATTLED over the roads on their way to Yardley Hall, Surrey where the Marquess of Aaron and Cecilia had invited a select group of guests to a fortnight long house party. The invitation had come the day after Katherine had experienced the most eye-opening kiss within the conservatory with Lord Leighton.

He wished to see her again, had promised to show her more, so would he act on that at Cecilia's country home. Trepidation and excitement thrummed through her at the thought and she shifted on the seat, enjoying the delicious ache it aroused at her core.

It was a novel experience being wanted, and she knew by his ardent response to her kiss he desired her. For heavens knew, she wanted him.

The carriage turned through the gates of Yardley Hall and Katherine looked down into the gully and saw the sprawling mansion, its glass windows twinkling in the afternoon sun. She'd been the last to leave London due to her work, as she'd needed to oversee the roof slates that were now going up on Lord Leighton's townhouse. The structural work was coming along very well, and soon their side of the building would be complete and her association with his lordship on a business side would be finished. She could only hope it wasn't the end of their personal one.

Before the house party invitation arriving she'd not been summoned by Lord Leighton and she consoled herself that it was simply because he'd see her here. They were not courting, he'd explained his reasonings behind that, and she had accepted them. He owed her, and he would pay that debt back in the most pleasurable way possible. After that, there was nothing more he expected.

The carriage moved down on the gravel road, weaving toward the estate and she lost sight of it a moment. She'd started to hope for something else. Something more. Unmarried and six and twenty, how could she not? This was likely her last chance of securing a gentleman who'd take her on. She pushed away the negative thoughts that wanted to mock her idea of landing the earl as a husband. Born into a family of builders, she might be from Cheapside, but she was a lady and had grown up with the best tutors and etiquette coaches. She might not have a title or be the daughter of a titled gentleman, but she was worthy and equal to them. In her own mind at least.

But would Lord Leighton see such things, or merely just wish to bed her and be done with it?

The carriage rocked to a halt and she startled so lost in thought. She waited for a footman to open the door and took his arm as she alighted. The afternoon sun bore down on this side of the home, and even though the slight wind was a little chilling, it was refreshing and invigorating being out of the carriage and out of the city.

The front door opened, and Cecilia came out, climbing down the couple of steps to hug her quickly before leading her indoors. "I'm so glad you were able to make it. You have been missed the last five days. I hope you were able to arrange it to return with us Wednesday next?"

"It's all arranged, and I have the time off, but I would so desperately love a bath. I had some last-minute paperwork to do this morning and so have come straight from the office."

"Of course, whatever you wish. I shall take you to your room immediately and send up some tea while they prepare you a bath. Dinner is served at eight sharp, and so once you are rested, we shall catch up more then."

"Thank you, Cecilia," she said, starting up the stairway. Making the first floor, they turned left along the extensive corridor and behind her Katherine could hear a multitude of voices and laughter. Was Lord Leighton in there, waiting for her?

"Maybe I ought to say hello first and then freshen up. I don't wish to be rude."

Cecilia ordered the servants to prepare a bath and refreshments and then took her arm, pulling her back toward the room the guests were gathered.

As much as she wanted to rest and refresh herself, the need to see Lord Leighton, to ensure he was in attendance was too much to deny, and as they made their way toward the room, Cecilia talking about the tidbits of gossip she'd heard the past five days, the entertaining nights and fun they'd had, caused nerves to settle in the pit of Katherine's belly.

They entered the room, and Darcy stood, coming over and kissing her cheek in welcome.

"We're so glad you've arrived. We almost expired of despair when you never came yesterday as planned. We thought you hadn't been able to get away."

Katherine smiled at some of the guests who acknowledged her and taking stock of the room quickly she noted one guest in particular who was missing. Her disappointment must have shown, for Cecilia tightened her grip on her arm, squeezing it a little.

"There are other guests of course. Lord Leighton is out riding with Lady Georgina Savile. They've become fast friends these past days, much in common with their mutual love of travel. I believe Lady Oliver mentioned her in London some weeks past. She's recently returned from abroad, Egypt in fact. She's particularly funny and smart.

And at that precise moment she entered the room, clasped tightly upon Lord Leighton's arm, both of them chuckling on some unknown amusing discussion the rest of the room was not privy to. The woman was everything Katherine was not, and if the world had opened at that moment and swallowed her whole, she would've been thankful.

Lady Savile had rich auburn hair, and skin as soft and pure as milk. If she had travelled abroad, Egypt in fact, she'd certainly taken care not to freckle or brown. Her breasts filled out her green riding gown to perfection, and her cheeks held the slightest shade of rose after their exertions on the horses. She wasn't as tall as Katherine, but not many women were, and she was also not as thin. In one word, the woman was beyond beautiful and it was no wonder Lord Leighton had enjoyed himself these past five days. Who would not with such company?

Katherine was dowdy, her traveling gown was well worn and brown and did nothing for her lifeless coloured hair. Her breasts didn't come up half to snuff of those of Lady Savile's and she could've cried regretting her decision to come and say hello to everyone before making herself more presentable.

What would most of these guests care that she was here? She was nothing but serving class to them. "Do you think my bath would be ready by now," she asked, Cecilia quietly. "I think I shall return to my room."

Darcy's gaze slid to Lord Leighton's and Katherine didn't miss the exchange. Lord Leighton made past them and nodded slightly in her direction, wishing her welcome before he sat down on a settee, a servant handing him and Lady Savile a glass of wine.

Katherine excused herself and left, Cecilia following close on her heels. "Is everything well, Kat. You seem upset?"

"I'm merely tired. I'm going to go rest a while, have my bath and put myself to rights. I shall see you at dinner." And then, once she was recovered, she would figure out a way to tell her friends that she would return to London. She didn't belong here, and she could never compete with a woman of Lady Savile's beauty and poise. And she didn't want to.

Lord Leighton hadn't seemed the least interested in her. It should not surprise her since he was famous about town for being a rake, easily bored and distracted. Perhaps it was best that she didn't follow through with her plan to lay with him. If the jealousy she now felt was any indication, she didn't need that to be one-hundred fold after knowing him intimately. The thought of his losing interest in her, maybe even finding a woman he wished to marry left a hollow sensation in the location her heart should sit. Such a notion would be unbearable.

CHAPTER 8

Hamish sat at table that evening, his attention snapping to Katherine with any opportunity. How beautiful she'd looked this afternoon after her arrival. Her hair had fallen down a little during her carriage ride to Yardley Hall, and her eyes were alight with possibility when talking to Cecilia and the duchess. That was, until she'd seen him with Lady Savile and all enjoyment, pleasure of being at the country house had vanished from her features. She'd looked devastated, if one could look such a way, and he'd cursed himself as a fool for being the one who'd put that look of disappointment in her rich brown eyes.

Lady Savile was a very beautiful woman, and certainly had he not known Katherine the way he did now, he might have tried his luck with the lady, but that wasn't the case now. He wasn't interested at all in the woman, only that of a friend, and before the night was out he'd make sure Katherine knew that fact too. He would not allow her to spend even one night fretting over something that didn't exist.

To make matters worse, he was seated beside Lady Savile who unknowingly with her amusing countenance, and their new friendship had no idea that the small touches she placed on his arm, her chuckling banter during dinner was causing the woman he cared for, more than he'd known up until he'd seen the hurt in her eyes this afternoon, more pain than he ever wished to imbue on her.

Damn it, he inwardly swore. As the dinner progressed, he didn't fail to miss that Katherine grew more and more quiet, refused to meet his gaze or converse in any conversation he was part of.

"Shall we play a game after dinner. I know of one that I think will be such fun," Lady Savile said, beaming at everyone, her jovial charm making the gentleman present enthusiastic and the women more so. All except Katherine who sipped her wine without comment.

"What a wonderful idea," Cecilia said, more than happy to get in on the act.

"The house is large, with numerous rooms and corridors, attics and cellars. And tonight, you'll get to explore some of it, but there's a catch," Lady Savile said, standing now and meeting everyone's eye to gain their attention.

"Oh, do tell." Katherine's words dripped with sarcasm and the worried glance Cecilia threw her didn't seem to temper Miss Martin's growing annoyance.

Hamish knew the root cause for her ire, and it was him and his bad handling of her arrival. He'd hoped she would arrive today after missing her own arrival date the day before. Still, he'd hankered to get outdoors and had gone out on a horse ride, only at the stables running into Lady Savile who asked if she could join him since she wasn't familiar with the grounds. He'd not been able to refuse, and when he'd seen Katherine's carriage roll down the hill he'd turned back to the estate, eager to see her again.

Yet, the moment he'd walked into the room, he couldn't allow anyone to see just how impatient he'd been and so he'd nodded in welcome, and that was all. And now, it would seem, Katherine was annoyed.

"Tonight," her ladyship continued, "we're going to play a game of hide and seek. After dinner, you will find in the entrance hall a footman who has a pack of cards in a hat. They are all black, bar two. You will each be required to pull out a card. The black card will mean you hide, the white card will mean you are the seekers. For those who pick white cards, you must find as many people as you can within one hour. Whoever remains hidden and is not found, wins," she said, beaming with excitement.

Lady Savile resumed her seat, seemingly pleased with her instructions for the evening and Cecilia stood to speak. "You may continue with your dinner and we'll get onto our little game in a short while."

From there, dinner passed pleasantly, and as expected, the discussion turned to the game they were to play afterwards, each of them discussing what was in bounds and out about the house. By the time dinner had passed, Hamish was desperate to speak to Katherine. After her hasty departure to her room this afternoon, she'd not returned, and she'd been one of the last guests to arrive for dinner. That she was avoiding him was obvious, but he wouldn't allow it to continue. He hated the fact she'd been hurt by his actions. And he hated the fact that he'd tempered his reaction to seeing her all because it was what was expected.

With the dinner at an end, and the guests coming to stand in the entrance hall, as promised, a footman waited for them all, holding a black beaver. A few of the women tittered in excitement. Was it because they were to explore

the home, full of hidden passageways and secret compart-
ments, or merely the possibility of finding oneself alone
with a gentleman admirer.

Hamish waited back, wanting to see if Katherine
would play at all, and because of the good humor from her
friends the duchess and marchioness, she pulled out a card.
It was a black card meaning she was to hide.

Hamish too took a card, it was white, before siding up
to Katherine, leaning close to ensure privacy. "Do not hide
too hard, Miss Martin. I'll not be able to find you."

This close, he felt the shiver that ran down her body, it
gave him hope that she wasn't through with him, had cast
him out as a swine and rogue.

"You forget, I've been here before, twice in fact, and I
know this house well. You'll never find me." She met his
challenging gaze with one of her own and heat shot threw
him. He wanted her. He wanted all of her and no one else.

Hamish grinned. "We will see, shall we not." He left
her, knowing full well as he made his way back into the
library she watched his every move.

❦

KATHERINE KNEW EXACTLY where she was going to hide
where no one would find her. The marquess and Cecilia's
home was a rabbit warren of rooms, corridors and hidden
passageways, one of which ran along the gallery wall.
Cecilia had shown her only the last time she was here. One
simply had to hold back the tapestry of knights in battle,
and a wooden door sat behind it. In fact, it wasn't even a
door, simply a door disguised as the wall panelling.

As she made her way up to the first floor, people ran
past her, men and women both, laughing, squealing in

delight. One or two even disappeared into rooms that were not part of the game. Katherine shrugged it off, and continued on to the gallery, happy to find that no one had followed her into this part of the house, which was sparsely lit and devoid of servants.

She found the tapestry and pulling it out a little, pushed on the panel behind. It opened with only the slightest creak and picking up a candelabra she slipped into the passage and closed the door. For a hidden passage it was reasonably clean, and someone had even placed a chair in the corridor. She would have to ask Cecilia if she'd done such a thing and why.

The sound of running footsteps outside and more laughter passed, and Katherine smiled. No one, not even Lord Leighton would find her in here. She supposed she might miss out on all the fun of being found being so well hidden, but it was too late now to change her mind. Not that she wished to be found by his lordship in any case. Today, he'd proven to her really what a silly numbskull she'd been to think he might possibly care for her more than he did. That he might actually like her for who and what she was, not simply because she asked him to deflower her.

Katherine shook her head, what a stupid fool she'd been. And it was not something she could take back. Even her friends knew of her idea regrettably. For the rest of her spinsterhood days, she would be thrown into his sphere simply because they had the same friends, and she would feel mortified each and every time. If only she had never asked him.

Footsteps sounded and stopped on the other side from where she sat. Katherine stilled, her heart surging in alarm. Surely no one knew where she was… The panelling pushed open and the dark head and teasing grin of Lord

Leighton came into view. He shut the panel behind him before he spoke, leaving them alone. Quite alone.

"How did you find me here?" Not sure if she was affronted by being found so easily or that the nerves coursing through her veins were due to them being solitary and in a darkened space to boot.

"The tapestry in the gallery was kinked. I walked through here earlier today, and it wasn't, and so I took a guess. And what a lucky guess it was."

He came to stand before her, for the first time in forever, he made her feel a little small. After all, he was taller than her by a good two inches, not many men could boast such a thing in either her social sphere or his. "You were lucky, and one would say I was unlucky. I suppose we'll have to return downstairs and you may boast that you found me."

His gaze dropped to her lips and stayed there. "Or, you could grant me a winner's boon."

"Such as?" Katherine had the overwhelming urge to pull out her fischu and use it as a fan. For a hidden corridor that ran in either direction and was long and winding, it was awfully hot and crowded in the space.

"Maybe you will grant me," he stepped even closer. "A ki–"

"I shall not kiss you, my lord. I find I'm not at liberty this evening."

He grinned and damn it, her heart fluttered. "*Not at liberty*. May I ask as to why you scorn me? I have not seen you this afternoon, nor before dinner. I had hoped to talk to you before we dined."

Katherine shrugged, and Hamish stepped back, the separation making her chest hurt.

"You're angry at me. Why?"

Something in his tone told her he already suspected,

but if she were to admit to her annoyance, her hurt, it would pave way to him knowing that she'd hoped for more. That she cared. And she would not have that. She would not be made a fool of twice.

"I made a mistake when I asked you to make love with me. I apologize, and I no longer wish to act on my curiosity. I'm sorry to have thrown myself at your head." Katherine went to move past him and he blocked her way.

"I'm not sorry that you asked me. Although I know you're aware I'm not seeking a wife, it does not mean with care that we cannot enjoy each other. No matter what you believe, Kat, for some weeks now you've become an important part of my life. You inspire me with your independence and your employment. You do not need a man to guide you through life, as you're your own woman. I admire you and I desire you." He stepped closer still and Katherine instinctively stepped back, only to come up hard against the wall. "I want you, no one else, no matter what you think you saw today, it was all a show. It is you that my heart beats hard for, that my body reacts to. It is you and only you that I want to warm my bed."

She swallowed, heat blooming on her cheeks, and she was thankful for the shadows about them. His words, thick and husky pulled at the part of her that was lonely, longing for a future that she thought lost. A moan rented the air, and Katherine jumped against him, clasping his lapels. "That sounded like what one would think was a ghost."

He chuckled, wrapping one arm about the curve of her back and a delicious shiver stole down her spine.

"I think it came from up here." He pulled her along. "Come, we will investigate further."

"I'm not sure that is wise. I don't want to see any of Lord Aaron's ancestors floating past me, thank you very much."

To her astonishment, he stopped and lifting her chin, kissed her. A gentle, feathered touch that shot straight to her heart. *Oh dear, she was on dangerous ground, and not because of the dark…*

"Do not fret, darling Kat. I shall save you."

Katherine leaned close to his side as they started down the corridor, the single candelabra their only light. The corridor remained straight for some time, following the portrait gallery outside before it made a sharp left.

There was no warning other than a curse that echoed off the walls as his lordship tripped over, their only form of light guttered in the process. She froze, not wanting to trip over too. "Are you alright, my lord."

"Hamish, please. No titles, it's too formal."

"Are you really worried about that now? Simply answer the question." She spoke into the darkness, not able to see anything at all.

More scratching and another curse. "Where the hell?"

Katherine gasped as one, large, male hand landed directly on her breast. Her body shot to life, and she hoped, even craved that his hand would curve about her aching flesh and squeeze it a little. Anything to save her from this throbbing need she had for him. "Hamish…"

His rapid breathing told her without sight that he reacted in kind and he took an awfully long time to remove his hand. "I should apologize. It's certainly what a gentleman should do."

Her breast ached with the lack of his touch when he pulled away, and she wasn't ready for him to stop touching her. But here and now wasn't the time for a rendezvous. The whole company at the home were playing a game, and should they go missing, especially Hamish as he was supposed to be finding other guests, it would cause a huge scandal.

"It was an accident, brought on by the fact we're stuck in a hidden passageway in pitch black. How on earth are we going to find our way back?" she said, hoping to change the subject. Around Lord Leighton she did not trust herself. Impulses he'd awoken refused to settle and demanded she do as she wanted, not what she ought.

"There, ahead of us," he said, his voice close. "There is a small light." His hand fluttered down her arm before he took her hand. "Let us take it slowly, less we both fall over next time."

She chuckled and let him lead the way. They walked slowly, more cautious now that their vision was impaired by the darkness, but the small light that they had spied wasn't a door at all, a small hole gave them view into the corridor, or what Katherine thought was the corridor at least.

The groan that they'd heard earlier sounded again and she clutched at his arm. Lord Leighton paused to look through the hole and cursed. "Do not look, Katherine. Come, we'll continue this way."

"What is it? What have you found?" She pushed him aside and standing on tiptoe she looked through the hole. It was something that Katherine had never seen before in her life and loathed to think that such a thing may be located in her room, as it was in this one.

"Oh my," she gasped, unable to look away from the vision before her. That of two of the guests, who came without partners following the death of their spouses were enjoying each other very much in private.

"Come, Kat."

His voice was strained, deeper than she'd heard it before and she cursed not being able to see him, see what the vision they'd just viewed was doing to him. "I'm glad they're enjoying themselves," she said, grinning at her own words.

"Are you not enjoying yourself?"

She reached out for his hand and her palm landed directly on his chest. He was all muscle, a virile healthy man. The only man who'd ever made her weak at the knees. "I would enjoy our time here more if we were doing what was happing right now in the room beside us."

In the dark, everything seemed magnified, his breathing, her shivers as his hand came up to cover hers sitting on his chest. After seeing him today with Lady Savile she'd not thought she would ever feel jealousy, hurt even inflicted by someone else, but thinking of Hamish in the arms of another woman, loving her as she wanted left a hollow in her heart.

She bit her lip. Would he do as she asked, as they'd agreed, or since being here, meeting a women who suited his tastes more, both in looks and social standing, did he simply not want her?

He pulled her into his arms, and a small flutter went off in her stomach. "If you will have me, Katherine, I will come to your room tonight. I've already found out which one it is. And then my dearest," he said, his hands bracketing her face and kissing her. "We shall do everything you want."

Heat pooled between her legs and she moaned when he kissed her again. The thought of them doing what she'd seen the couple undertaking through the peep hole left her longing for the night to end so theirs could begin.

"Anything?" Katherine hadn't been shy about reading up on what lovers partook during a sexual act, and there were some very interesting ideas that she longed to try. But would he let her? Excitement thrummed through her veins. She supposed she was to soon find out. If this was her one and only night with Lord Leighton, then she would make the most of it.

He chuckled, pulling her back along the passage. "I'm yours to do with as you wish, but first, we have to find a way out of this infernal passage. If I don't return you soon to company, I cannot be held responsible for my actions. Not even in this black hole."

CHAPTER 9

Hamish paced back and forth in his room, waiting for the house to quieten after the night's activities. The game had continued after Katherine and he had found their way out of the secret passageway, and with her help, he'd found most of the guests. After that, the party gathered in the music room downstairs for cards, some dancing and good conversations.

Yet, the entire time, all Hamish could think about was what was to come. He wanted to make Katherine's first time a pleasurable one and he'd gone over in his mind again and again what he could do to ensure that.

It was not the best course of action since he was in company at the time, and would not, under any circumstances stand to converse. Katherine had mingled for the remainder of the night, and after their talk upstairs, she seemed to have mellowed a little around Lady Savile and yet, every now and then he caught sight of her admiring the woman and a little alarm went off in his mind.

Did she think she was not as attractive, not as beautiful as the other women that were present? To him, Katherine was the most beautiful woman he'd ever met, and after tonight she would know that.

He checked the time, it was past one and still he could hear people out in the corridor, guests heading for bed. Finally. Some minutes later, his door opened, and he turned to see Katherine slip inside and close it quickly. She turned to him, a silk dressing robe over her shift. He let out a pained breath. Damn it, she was beautiful, and his. His to adore and to cherish for the night.

"You took too long, Lord Leighton. I hope you've not changed your mind," she said, coming toward him and sliding off her robe, only to throw it on a nearby chair.

Hamish found his voice, although even to himself he sounded breathless. When had she become an expert siren? He met her half way and pulling her into his arms he kissed her, like he'd wanted to kiss her when he'd entered the parlor this afternoon after his ride.

She melted against him, all soft womanly flesh that sent his wits spiralling. He ran his hands over her back, over her buttocks to pull her hard against his bulging cock that strained against his breeches. That she was here, in his room, and they were alone, wouldn't be disturbed all night, sent his pulse to gallop.

He nibbled her lips, explored her mouth with his tongue, groaned when she matched him, stroke for stroke, touch for touch.

"Katherine," he whispered against her neck, nipping on the little vein that protruded there. Her skin smelt of soap, and jasmine, her hair of fruits. He had no doubt she'd taste just as good.

Hamish couldn't wait much longer to see her, he wanted to gaze down upon her full glory and revel in it.

She broke the kiss and stepped back, holding his gaze, hers heavy with desire that shot blood straight to his groin.

Katherine stood before him, her shift almost translucent and pulled the small ties at the front of her gown apart. He could not pull his attention away from her hands, or what they were doing for anything, and then, with a lift of her shoulder and little shimmy the shift dropped and pooled about her feet.

Underneath she was gloriously naked. Hamish reached out and traced her collarbone, her audible gasp almost put an end to his resolve to look, to admire and learn every ounce of her. Her breasts, which were larger than he'd thought rose with every breath, her nipples the sweetest pink he'd ever beheld, and puckered into tight buds.

He wanted to lick them, suckle and kiss them until she was writhing and begging for him. He licked his lips, imaging it, all the while knowing that within a few moments he'd be doing what he'd wanted to for weeks. His gaze moved downwards to her perfect waist, and hips that flared. She was so beautiful his breath caught in his lungs.

"You do me such an honor, Katherine." He grazed his hand over her navel and meeting her gaze, moved it down to cup between her legs. She was gloriously wet, ready for him.

Her hands came about his neck and she cried out, the sound breaking the little control he held. Swinging her up in his arms, he walked them to the bed, laying her down and coming to lie over her. She shook beneath him, and he kissed her, wanting to dispel any nerves. If he could help it he would never hurt her, but if there were the slightest pain during their joining it would be minimal and soon replaced with pleasure.

Katherine positively trembled with want of Hamish.

His strong, lean, muscular body over hers, the wisp of hair that tickled her breasts, the slight grazing of his stubbled jaw as he kissed her, conquered her mouth in a punishing kiss. Katherine promised herself then and there should she never have another such kiss her life would be content. For to have such a kiss from Hamish, one that told her without words that she was wanted, desired, longed for, was more than anything she'd ever expected.

His hands clasped her thigh and he lifted her leg to sit against his hip. The position allowed him to press himself against her fully, and all her thoughts centered on the one place that begged, throbbed for more.

"What is this madness you're doing to me," she gasped, watching him as he kissed his way down her chest to only stop at her breasts and look at them. Katherine fought not to hide herself, conscious of the fact that she wasn't as full in the breast area than his usual lovers, but his exquisite unbidden delight when looking at them seemed to say he didn't mind. One hand cupped her breast and pleasure rocked through her. He leaned down, licking first her nipple before giving it a teasing nip.

She moaned, a sound that mingled with his own groan. Katherine pushed up against him, his hard member solid against her core and she ached so very much to have it inside her. Although she'd never experienced such things before, surely it would feel as good as his mouth on her now.

He moved to lavish attention to the other breast, and she speared her fingers through his hair, holding him against her so he might never stop his attentions. His hand slid down her stomach, clasping her there before delving between her wet folds.

Katherine shut her eyes as he slid his fingers against her most private of places, using his thumb to roll against a part of her that made her want nothing but him. "Hamish," was all she could manage to say while her mind whirred. Was it like this always between married couples? To know this kind of pleasure would be unbearably hard to only experience once.

He groaned and kissed his way down her stomach. So, lost in her own enjoyment she didn't realize what he was doing before his heated breath caressed her mons. She attempted to sit up, but he merely met her gaze, a feral edge to it that made her flustered and warm, before pushing on her stomach, warning her to stay.

"Lay back and relax. If we're to only have one night, we're going to have a long and very varied one." He bent his head and Katherine sighed, biting her lip as his mouth, his tongue...What his tongue was doing was beyond anything she'd ever thought. When she'd seen such draw-ings in the books she'd borrowed from the Duke of Athel-by's library, she never imagined how wonderful it would feel.

He slid a finger across the spot that thrilled with every touch and then slid it inside.

"Damn Kat, you're so tight."

Katherine was beyond thought or words, she simply clung onto his head, holding him, undulating against his face like a woman gone wild. How had she not known it could be like this with a man. How could she ever move forward in life and only have this once.

Only make love with Hamish once...

His ministrations continued, with every thrust of his hand, his tongue matched its purpose and with agonising delight, her body coiled, thrived on his touch and sought something she'd never known.

"That's it darling, let go. Come for me," he said, kissing her again without restraint. His teasing lightened to a slow torment and her body hitched, her hips pushing up to find release. Without any care as to how wanton she might seem, pleasure like none she'd ever known rocked through her body. Tremor after tremor of delicious spasm ran across her skin and she giggled, her limbs weak, her body slackened and sated.

Hamish kissed his way up her body, hitching her leg over his hip. "My turn," he said, kissing her deeply.

She tasted herself on him, and it sent the beginnings of pleasure to build once again. This is what she wanted after all. To have Hamish just like this, her lover, a man who for one night at least would worship her body, make her feel just as beautiful as anyone else.

He positioned himself at her opening. "I'm sorry, my darling, this may be uncomfortable." He thrust forward and Katherine gasped at the sting of pain, clutching at his shoulders. He stopped moving, and simply stayed fully lodged within her. It allowed her to get used to the feeling of him being there, inside her.

It was odd, there was no doubt about that, but when he moved again, instead of pain there was only the residual delight of her own release, doubly so, now that Hamish was going to experience the same.

He pushed into her, groaning against her neck when she lifted her legs higher.

"You're so beautiful, Katherine," he rasped against her lips, watching her as he took her. His arms strained as he held himself atop her, his corded muscles straining with the effort and never had she seen anything so desirous in all her life.

His strokes became faster, harder and she found the more he took her like this, the more her body craved release. She was becoming a woman who couldn't get enough of him, and one night seemed such a waste. Surely, they could have two.

"Katherine," he moaned, taking her lips, his hips flexing. Warmth spread through her, and at the last minute he pulled out, spilling his seed across her stomach. Hamish collapsed beside her, and reaching into the bedside cabinet drawer, he pulled out a cloth and wiped her clean before drawing her up against his chest. "We shall rest for a time, and then my dear, I will show you what else we can do."

His teasing grin mimicked her own. "There's more we can do?" The idea never occurred to her, not really. She'd seen images in books, but she'd always assumed those positions were exotic, not performed by well-bred English lords. Excitement thrummed through her as one image she wanted to try came to mind.

"You look positively naughty. What is going on in your mind?" he asked, kissing her so gently on the lips that her heart gave a flip.

She leaned up and whispered her thought in his ear, unable to voice it out loud, even though they were quite alone. His eyes went wide, before they darkened in hunger. He rolled her over onto her back, pinning her to the bed.

"Are you sure?" he asked, his body tight and his manhood hard again against her leg.

She nodded, her body wiggling in renewed need. "Oh yes, I'm sure. Show me everything."

He growled. "With pleasure."

CHAPTER 10

Katherine sat in the morning room alone. Before her was an untouched pot of tea and an assortment of cakes. She stared at the little flowery design on the side of the teapot and thought about what had transpired between her and Lord Leighton last night. Actually, even this morning if she were honest about their interlude. It had been quite vigorous and lengthy and very much enlightening. She grinned. How different she felt now that she'd slept with a man. Wiser in her wisdom, certainly wiser as to what she'd been missing all these years. Silly dolt.

She kicked her legs out from beneath her and poured herself a cup. Limiting her milk so the tea wasn't too cold, she took a small sip, relaxing back in her chair. When they'd parted this morning, a quick chaste kiss in the corridor there had been no mention of any more nights. Would he stick to their agreement of only one night together? They seemed to get along very well in private, and it would be a shame to stop it since it really had only just begun.

"Oh, here you are, my dear. I've been looking all over

for you." Katherine smiled as Cecilia bustled into the room, her morning gown of white embroidered cotton making her look like a summer's dream. Marriage seemed to suit her friend very well, and if the glow on her cheeks was any indication, she got along quite well with Lord Aaron in private too.

"I'm just having a cup of tea, before I'm to head outdoors to join in the game of croquet you have set up outside. Do you care to join me?"

"I'd love to. After all the running about this morning I'm in need of substance." Cecilia sat, her golden locks were pulled up high on her head, and yet a few wisps framed her pretty face.

"You do look like you've been busy. Can I help you with anything?" Katherine asked, sitting back in her chair and taking another sip.

Cecilia busied herself pouring a cup of tea and picking up a small biscuit. "No, everything is under control, but I would like to know what happened last evening with Lord Leighton."

Katherine coughed, choking on her tea. "I'm sorry. What?" How did she know? When she'd snuck into his room she was very discreet and had made sure the last of the guests had gone to their rooms before she scuttled down the passage way to his suite.

Cecilia raised a knowing brow. "He's outside partaking in the games and seems quite jovial this morning. In fact, the poor fellow keeps looking back at the house as if he's expecting someone and it made me wonder. Especially when everyone who's here for the fortnight is outside on the lawns. All but one."

Pleasure ran through her veins. Was Hamish looking for her? Waiting for her? "These cakes are delicious,

Cecilia. You must give my regards to your cook when you see her next."

Cecilia wagged her finger, grinning. "Oh, no you don't. You're going to tell me Kat what you've done under this roof, if only so I can be there for you. Support you in your choice."

Katherine stood and walked to the window to look out onto the back grounds. Sure enough, in buckskin breeches and a day coat of bottle green stood Lord Leighton, deep in conversation with his friend Lord Bridgman. The game made him take a couple of steps, and it was only then that Katherine was reminded of his lean form, his strong arms and very darling bottom.

She turned and faced her oldest friend. "I slept with Lord Leighton and worse," she said pausing. "I want to do it again."

Cecilia's eyes went wide, and she placed her tea cup down. "Come and sit. This we need to discuss at length."

Katherine did as she was asked, folding her hands in her lap as she waited for Cecilia to either condone or condemn her. She hoped it would the former.

"I did not think that Lord Leighton wished to have such intimate relations with you. What changed his mind?" Cecilia asked, her gaze trained on her with unwavering focus and concern.

She shrugged. "I suppose it has something to do with the fact that whenever we're together the feelings, the desire that we both feel overrides what our decisions should be. I will never marry, at my age it's too late for me, and I know I'm also not the kind of woman that Lord Leighton has normally chased. Not that he chased me, but I do not fit his ideal mould." Tears pricked her eyes, and she sniffed, unsure where all this overwhelming emotion was coming from. Did all woman cry after a night of bliss? Surely not.

"We parted on good terms, but no mention was made on continuing our liaison. And so, it seems that perhaps he has held up to his end of the bargain by giving me the one thing that I wished and that is that. But I hope it's not the case. I like him," she stated. It was the truth after all. "I like him a lot."

"Oh, Katherine," Cecilia said, coming to sit beside her. "Do not despair, not yet at least. Today is a new day, and such liaisons between two unmarried people is highly scandalous, so he will not be forward in his regard with you, not in public. You may find today when you do speak to him, that he feels the same way and wishes a courtship with you. I can have Hunter have a word with him if you like. Remind Lord Leighton of his honor as a gentleman to not dally with unmarried women only to kick them aside when he's had his fill."

Katherine shook her head, hating even the thought of others telling Lord Leighton what he ought to do simply because of what they'd done. After all, it was her idea to have him sleep with her. "Please don't. I'm sure no matter what transpires today, Lord Leighton and myself will remain friends. I was the one who instigated all of this in the first place, you cannot have someone chastise him simply because I teased him until he did as I wished." What a conundrum she was in. And one of her own making.

"Let us join the others outside. I'm merely being foolish hiding away indoors." Katherine stood. "Shall we?"

Cecilia expelled a resigned sigh but stood. "Very well, but please confide in me if anything troubles you. I want you to be happy above anything else."

Katherine hugged Cecilia to her as they walked out onto the terrace and made their way down the stairs and onto the large expanse of lawn. "I will come to you should anything upsetting occur, but until then, please don't fret over me. I'm older than you remember. I'm perfectly well and capable of handling my life."

"I know you are."

Darcy waved and came over to join them, and for a moment the three simply stood and watched some of the guests play croquet. The players' laughter during the game brought a smile to Katherine's lips and she found herself forgetting her troubles over what to do with Hamish and simply enjoyed the house party.

Lord Leighton took a shot and the small white ball went through the hoop, giving him the lead. He whooped, laughing and smiling at his good fortune. She sighed at how good looking he was, especially compared to her. She wasn't foolish enough that she believed herself a great beauty, not when Lady Savile walked up to Hamish, placing her hand on his arm as they laughed about something going on in the game.

"It is harmless, Kat. Lady Savile is simply flirtatious by nature. She's not interested in Lord Leighton. I promise you that."

Katherine looked back toward the pair, and caught Hamish watching her, leaning casually against his croquet stick, his dark hooded eyes raking over her in a way that her skin prickled in heat.

"And from that look," Darcy said, chuckling a little. "He's not interested in Lady Savile either, but in fact, another woman altogether."

Her stomach twisted in knots and she smiled a little.

The game ended and as Hamish started in her direction, Darcy and Cecilia joined their husbands who were seated at an outdoor table, fully engaged in what looked to be a very loud and engaging debate over Tattersalls' upcoming sale.

"Are you not going to congratulate me, Miss Martin? I won."

Katherine raised her brow, nerves fluttering in her belly knowing this was the first time they'd spoken since last night. A night where he'd shown her a great many things a woman and man could do, that even now made her ache. Would he be willing to continue their liaison? Could she trust that what she suspected of him, his liking of her, and his need were real, and not just because she'd been desperate and begged him to make love to her?

"Congratulations," she said, "you must be very proud." Katherine smiled, ignoring the fact that all she wanted to do right now was fling herself into his arms and kiss him.

He checked the whereabouts of the other guests before he said, "Is that all I'm to receive from you? Nothing else you're willing to give to the winner?"

"I do not understand your meaning, my lord," she said, trying not to look at his full lips that again reminded her of where they been last night on her person, and the pleasure they'd wrought. She failed utterly. His hair was tied back, but in the outdoors little wisps floated about his face. Last night she'd clasped his hair, holding him as she'd kissed him to distraction. She wanted to see him in such a way again.

"Tell me, Miss Martin, what do you think would be a fitting prize for a gentleman such as myself. A bottle of the finest whisky? A few sovereigns to line my pocket." He leaned toward her. "A kiss from the woman who keeps me up all night for want of her?"

She shivered, knowing that if they were to kiss, the embrace would lead to so much more. The duke of Athelby and the Marquess called out to Hamish to come and join their new croquet game. Hamish waved to them over his shoulder, yelling out, "Just a minute."

"You want to kiss me again, my lord. I thought after last night our agreement has been completed and you're free from any obligation to me." Her stomach roiled at voicing her fears, that what she actually said was true. Would he agree, turn from her and move on to his next lover? Someone more positioned in Society, more to his tastes and desires.

"I want to do a lot more than kiss you, Kat. I know our interlude was only meant to be one night, but it's not enough. Not enough for me and I hope for you too." He walked them along the lawn, giving the illusion that they were simply strolling and enjoying the day. "There is a hot spring here on the Marquess's lands. I will come to you tonight, and we shall go there."

"I don't know if you've noticed, Hamish, but it isn't very warm. We shall freeze."

He chuckled, his free hand coming to rest atop hers that sat on his arm. "I'll keep you warm," and with those words he threw her a devilish grin and joined the duke and marquess.

Katherine could do little but stare after him. He wasn't finished with her. He wanted to spend more time with her, just as she'd hoped.

She'd never been desired by a man before, and it was a mix of trepidation and exhilaration that Lord Leighton did. Katherine held no illusions that this liaison would go anywhere, but she'd asked to know what life would be like with a man, and he was going to show her, and no matter the risks she would jump into the void and revel in it.

CHAPTER 11

L ater that night they crept out of the house and stole across the lawns down toward the river that ran through the Marquess of Aaron's estate. The night was bright thanks to the full moon and very little clouds, although in the distance Hamish could see the flash of lightening and hear the low rumble of thunder.

The hot spring was a fortunate addition to the estate, and many years ago, the Marquess's grandfather had the spring transformed into a location family and guests could use. Today the spring was lined with stone, and housed paving about the edges, so people could get in and out without making their feet dirty. Inside the spring there was a ledge that ran along the outer edges of the circular bath, giving those enjoying the warm water a seat to sit on while partially submerged.

"Oh my, this is amazing," Katherine said, as the path gave way to the spring.

Steam rose into the night sky, and the closer they came toward it, the warmer the air became.

"If I were Cecilia I would live in this." She let go of his

hand and went over to the water, dipping her hand into it. "It's so hot."

A condition that Hamish was feeling most decidedly as well. Seeing Katherine under a moonlit sky, her skin translucent and flushed after their exertion of running toward the spring, left an odd ache in his chest. He untied his cravat, laying it on a bench that sat beside the spring. "Shall we get in?" he asked, removing his waistcoat.

Katherine joined him. He sucked in an audible breath when she clasped his shirt and pulled it over his head. "Most definitely."

They undressed quickly, both helping the other with buttons and ties. Hamish stood back and watched as she dropped her shift about her legs, her figure more magnificent than he'd ever thought possible. He'd not thought he would ever want a woman as much as he wanted Katherine, and the emotion gave him pause. To feel more for someone other than merely like was dangerous ground. Such emotions led to marriage and then children, and the latter was an affliction that he would never submit his bride to. The woman he married would not want children. He had his heir, and he would not risk the life of his wife simply to have child. He'd already lost a sister, that was well and truly enough.

Her hand clasped his jaw, and he met her gaze, surprised to see concern in her rich brown orbs. "Is everything well, Hamish? You seem a little lost in thought."

He pulled her into his arms, kissing her soundly. She chuckled through the kiss, before her arms came about his neck and she kissed him back with as much passion as she brought forth in him. Scooping her into his arms, he carried her into the spring, stepping down into the water with care. Releasing her, he allowed her to gain her feet, and watched in delight as she waded into the hot water.

"Oh, it's heavenly. Thank you for bringing me here." She kneeled into the water, covering her body and he missed her puckered nipples that had reacted to the cold night air.

Hamish went and sat on the bench, watching her as she floated about in the water, simply enjoying their time there before she joined him on the seat. She slid her hands up his chest and kissed him quickly on the lips.

"Now that you have me here, all alone and...naked, what are we going to do?"

Her grin was infectious, and he chuckled. "What did you have in mind?" Hamish knew what he had in mind, what he'd thought of all day and nothing else. When Katherine had played croquet, she had bent over to hit the little white ball he'd been decidedly conscious of the fact his buckskin breeches and day coat could only cover so much of his desire for her. He'd had to sit himself down and talk about London's latest *on dit* just to distract himself. "Maybe you ought to straddle my lap, and we'll go from there."

Her eyes brightened with interest and she quickly did as he suggested. Her body fit him like a glove, smooth and silky in his hands. Her mons pressed against his cock and she sighed when she purposefully slid against him, her gaze darkening in arousal.

"And now what?" she asked, running her hands into his hair and holding him tight. Her breathing deepened, and he could see that her continual sliding against his rock-hard member was giving her pleasure, teasing her to do more.

"Now," he said, his voice taut. "You'll guide me within you. And then, my darling." He ran his hand along her spine to clasp her nape. "You're going to fuck me."

She half gasped half moaned, and the idea of what

he'd said threatened his sanity. She reached between them, and clasping his cock, moving it toward her cunny.

Katherine bit her lip , and with a torturously slow descent, she took him fully within her. Her eyes widened before hunger crossed her features. "I thought it would hurt."

He shook his head, holding her hips and guiding her into a steady rhythm. "If we're doing it right, it will never hurt again."

Something shifted in her eyes before she blinked, and it was gone. She moved more forcefully and all thoughts of anything else vanished from his mind. He would have her like this for as long as she wished it. He could not give her up. "I knew one night with you would never have been enough."

She shivered in his hold before she kissed him with sensuous heat. He reveled in the arms of a woman who wasn't afraid to take or ask for what she wanted. To give her the control to take their lovemaking at her own pace. While it might drive him to insanity, he would ensure she gained her pleasure before he would take his.

Katherine arced her back, giving him a beautiful view of her breasts that rocked in the water. "You're so beautiful." He clasped one breast and leaning down kissed the rosy pink nipple. She moaned, increasing her pace and he fought for control. Damn it, he wanted to fuck her hard, sit her on the side of the spring, lay her down on the pavement and take her with his mouth. Wring every little amount of joy that he could while they were here, away from London and their normal lives.

Her core tightened about him, her pace increased, deepened and he groaned. "Yes, like that," he said, helping her to keep her rhythm.

Katherine shut her eyes, threw back her head as she

climaxed in his arms. Her satisfied sigh distracted him and at the peak of coming, he pulled out, wrapping his hand about his cock and pulled himself to climax.

She flopped against his chest and he held her close, running his hand along her back while they both regained their breaths.

"London will be so very boring when we return. Now that I've had you, how will I ever continue the life I had before? You've opened my eyes to what I've given up on, what I thought I didn't need," she murmured.

She laid her head against his shoulder and he met her gaze, leaning down to kiss her. He too wasn't unaffected by their joining. Hamish had never had an emotional reaction to having a woman before, he'd never had an overwhelming need to protect, to worry and care about her thoughts, needs and desires. His past liaisons had simply been sterile, non-emotional contacts. But with Katherine, something was different. He was different with her.

He liked her. A lot.

"Tell me something that you've never told another soul," he asked, wanting to know her better.

Her hand idly ran through his hair and she sighed. "I lied to you when I told you I wear breeches to work. I never wear them and had my father found out about my attire I would've been locked in my room until I expired of old age."

Hamish chuckled, not expecting that declaration of honesty. "You were very comfortable in them. What made you do it?"

"I found out you were to be at the house that day and I wanted to shock you, tease you even."

His hands ran down her back, sliding over one globe of her ass and his cock twitched. "Well, it worked. As I watched you walk up the stairs I thought of nothing other than whipping you into a vacant room, and removing those breeches."

"Really," she said, leaning up and kissing him.

Yes, really.

His heart thumped hard in his chest. "Maybe we could continue our affair in London, Katherine." He was a cad, he should never ask her to continue such an affair. The risk was all hers being unmarried and not his social equal. But he could not help himself. There was no doubt their paths would cross in London, their mutual friends ensured that. How could he turn away from her, not want her every time they met.

It would be torture and he couldn't do it. A warning gong sounded in his mind that he was going against his own rules, but at this moment, with the thought of not having Katherine in his arms again, just as she was now wasn't appealing. Hamish shoved the rules aside. They would simply have to be careful, both with not being caught and not getting her with child.

Her hand fluttered against his chest, settling over his heart. "You want that?"

He nodded without hesitation. "I do. You are not rid of me yet, Miss Martin, and until you've had your fill of me, that is how things will stay."

She sat up, squirming against him again. "What else can we do, Lord Leighton. I'm yours."

Her words rang with sincerity and spiked his lust. What was so different about her? What made her so special. "You're playing with fire, Katherine. Are you sure you want to know?"

She chuckled, her breasts grazing his chest and hardening his cock to rock. "Oh yes, I want to know and do everything before our time is up."

The thought of not having her this way, then watching

her walk out of his life and being only an acquaintance left a sour taste in his mouth. He would have her, care for her for as long as she wished him to. He hoisted her onto the side of the spring, sliding his hands against her thighs. "Lay back and open your legs. I want to taste you."

She bit her lip and he inwardly groaned. "If I do as you ask, can you promise me you'll allow me to do the same to you?"

Last evening she'd touched his cock, stroked it with her hand, but he'd not allowed anything else for fear of losing all control. The thought of her having her beautiful lips wrapped about his member, suckling hard, her tongue licking up his member almost made his eyes roll back in his head. "Very well, but first, it's my turn."

Katherine did as he asked. "Teach me," she said, sighing as he kissed her mons.

Oh, he intended to.

CHAPTER 12

Hamish sat in the library at his mother's townhouse, a pile of paperwork on his desk, some of which related to the rebuilding of his townhouse in Berkley Square. The letter, scrawled in delicate hand was signed by Katherine's father, but Hamish knew she'd written every word.

Since their return to London a month past, they had been inseparable, stealing away at events, coming together at nights when he'd take her home from balls and parties. He couldn't wait for his home to be completed so he could take her there instead, have her in his own bed and not a bloody carriage or room at a ball or party.

Hamish hadn't delved too much into what Katherine had come to mean to him, but what he did know was that he cared for her more than he'd cared for anyone else. Her happiness was paramount in his life, and that she still met his desire with as much eagerness as she did told him more than words ever could that they suited.

A knock sounded on his door, and he placed down Katherine's letter telling him that the construction part of his property was now complete, and the interior would commence, handled by Mr. Thomas Hope. It was a letter stating that her father's part in the reconstruction of his home was at an end and that payment would be due.

"Enter," he said, not liking the thought of going back to Berkley Square and not seeing Katherine there, dressed in breeches, the small grey cap perched jauntily atop her hair and looking so delectable that he'd had to steal her away one day and have her. He'd managed to lock them in his dining room where he'd taken her on the table. Never would he ever look at the mahogany set with anything but fondness.

"May I come in, Lord Leighton?" Lizzie stood at the door. He gestured her to come in.

"Have a seat, Lizzie." She did as he bade, and he gave her his full attention. "How can I help you?"

She clasped her hands tight in her lap, and her wringing of them gave her anxiety away.

"What troubles you?" he asked, placing down his quill.

Tears sprang into her eyes and he balked, not used to such feminine theatrics. Katherine never lost her countenance, she was calm and collected with everything. All except their lovemaking. He shook the thoughts aside and concentrated on Lizzie and her problem.

"Your mother wishes for us to marry my lord and I didn't know who else to turn to. For weeks she has been pushing me to gain your favour, but this time she's gone too far, and I cannot do it."

Hamish clenched his jaw not surprised Lizzie's upset was caused by his meddling parent. "What has she asked of you?" He hated to know, but if he was going to deal with the situation, and his mother in particular, he needed to know everything.

"She wanted me to be caught in your arms, near ruin

me so you would, as a gentleman, have to offer for me. I cannot do it, my lord. As much as I respect you and thank you for your service during the season, I do only feel brotherly affections for you."

After her impassioned speech, Hamish had to admit for a new-found respect for Miss Doherty. He'd thought her his mother's pawn and creature, but the girl had spunk, a little independent will and he liked that. She would need her backbone when his mother learned of her treachery.

"I thank you for being honest and notifying me of my mother's less than proper proposition. I shall speak to her and I can assure you, you will finish out the season without any influence from her or what her wishes are."

The girl pulled out a handkerchief and dabbed at her cheeks. "She'll send me back to the country where I shall die an old maid and never have what so many of my friends do."

The notion made him think of Katherine and the fact that at six and twenty she was termed old maid already and well on the shelf. The idea didn't sit well with him, never had. A woman of such independence of mind, a beautiful soul inside and out should never sit on a shelf and die an old maid, never loved or cherished.

"I promise you, that will never happen. And surely, there are men closer to you in age that have caught your attention. You will not pass away an old maid."

"I have no dowry, my lord. My father has settled everything on my brother and all that's left for me is a measly two-hundred pounds per year gifted to my husband upon my marriage. I may have admirers already, but I do not have the money to tempt them to propose. I seem to be only worth monetary value within our Society, not the value placed on myself."

She met his gaze, her words striking him as an unfortunate truth in their lives.

"I therefore shall never marry, for I cannot buy my husband," she said with a bitterness normally not seen in one so young.

Hamish stood, coming around the desk to lean on it before her. "I'll not allow that. Because you're under our protection, I shall ensure that such a thing will never happen. I will give you a dowry Miss Doherty. Ten thousand pounds in fact, a measly sum to my family, but, there is a condition."

"But my lord, I couldn't possibly. That's too much," she stammered, eyes flaring with shock.

"It is done. I shall have the papers drawn up by month's end, but as I said, there is a condition."

"And that is?" She'd paled, but she seemed to be listening.

"That we keep it a secret. And then, Lizzie, when you find the right gentleman, who'll love you as poor as you supposedly are, you'll know its love. You'll know that he is the right man for you."

She sat there for a moment, her mouth agape with no sound, before she jumped up, throwing her arms about him and hugging him tight. "Oh, thank you so much, Lord Leighton. Thank you so much. I shall be forever grateful and if you ever need anything, just say the word and I shall stand beside you always."

He set her back, shaking his head. "There is no need to thank me, you've paid penance enough for the dowry having to spend the season with my mother. Now," he said, pushing her toward the door, the paperwork on his desk waiting for no one. "Be on your way and enjoy what's left of the season, and don't be too quick to choose a husband.

Sometimes the one for you will arrive when you least expect it."

She nodded and quietly closed the door behind him. Hamish stared at it a moment, thinking of Katherine and how she had arrived in his life not at eighteen, and new to town, but at six and twenty, a woman, one who knew her mind, and wanted to know all that her body was capable of. A woman who worked for her living, and ran a very successful business.

Lizzie reminded him in many ways of his sister. Of her trepidation at having a London Season and trying to make a grand match. Luckily for May she'd married for love, a consolation considering she passed away giving birth to her other greatest love. He'd given his sister very similar advice that he'd given to Lizzie. To marry the man of her choosing, not that of their parent. After all, it was they who had to live with their choice when it was all said and done.

He smiled, thinking of Katherine. He would see her tonight at Lord and Lady Oliver's ball, the event of the season by all accounts. He would be returning to Hollyvale in a few weeks and the idea of leaving Katherine in town left a sour taste in his mouth. Would she come with him? If he invited their friends, perhaps she would, and then he could have her there, in his home, spend time with just her and no one else.

The word marriage flittered through his mind and he paused. Could he marry her, have a life with her? Panic tore through him at the thought of her getting with a child and dying. He could no longer deny what he felt for Katherine, for it was love, absolute, uncensored love, but he'd loved his sister too, and she had still died. Nothing could save her, other than the choice of not having children.

He doubted he'd be able to stop Katherine from wanting children and she deserved to be a mother, she didn't deserve to have his fears, his nightmares become her future. No, she deserved so much more than that.

CHAPTER 13

The ball was well under way, and Katherine had danced and laughed the night away with Cecilia and Darcy, along with Lord Leighton who hadn't left her side. He'd danced a waltz with her, stepped out with his mother's ward Miss Lizzie Doherty who seemed a lovely young woman, beside the fact she had to deal with Hamish's mother most days. Hamish had then danced with her again but seemed quite content not to move from his current position and dance with any others.

It suited Katherine perfectly well. She adored having him dote on her, and that's exactly what he'd been doing since their return from Surrey. Within their friendship group it was no longer a secret of their liaison. The duke had warned her of the scandal that would break should such a liaison become public knowledge. They'd been very discreet and careful and there was no reason why their relationship could not continue. At least in her mind.

Lord Leighton reached down between them and slid his finger over her pinkie. "Meet me in the music room. No one will be in there."

Need coursed through her veins and she met his gaze, reveling in the desire and heat that she saw there. He looked exactly how she felt. "Where is it?"

"Head toward the withdrawing room upstairs, but on the landing, turn right instead of left. It's the only door on the right-hand side of the corridor. I'll leave it ajar," he whispered, moving away through the throng.

Katherine made a point of taking little heed of his leaving and turned to Cecilia who was discussing the invitation Lord Leighton had bestowed on them all for a month-long house party at his country estate after the Season. Upon receiving the invite she'd thrilled at the idea of seeing his home, and yet, the thought gave her pause. They had been having an affair for almost two months and he had not once suggested as to when they would end, when he'd wish to leave.

And even though she'd asked him to sleep with her, show and teach her everything, it now felt like an arrangement, almost as if she'd become his mistress. Not that he wasn't caring, or loyal to her, for she never doubted that, only that she wanted more. Being loved by Hamish had showed her that she was valued as a woman, not just a Long Meg with plain hair that people passed over. But a woman, one who now knew how to love, not just Lord Leighton but herself. She did not dress to please anyone but herself, and she certainly carried herself as an equal with her friends. Never would she allow anyone to cast her out as if she was nothing but trade. But as time progressed, each liaison she had with Hamish had started to make her feel as if she wasn't worth more than a tumble. And it was no longer enough.

"I'm going to the retiring room. I shall be back shortly," she said, bobbing a small curtsy to her grace and the marquess and marchioness.

The room was easy to find and entering she quickly looked to ensure no one had seen her and shut the door. Hamish stood by the windows, looking out over the gardens. Her heart did a little flip and she took her fill of him before walking over to where he stood.

"You look so beautiful tonight," he said, kissing her. It had been almost two weeks since they'd seen each other, and the embrace quickly turned from sedate, and sweet to incendiary. Somehow, each time they were together they just worked. They knew where each other liked to be touched, what kisses drove the other mad, and Katherine clung to him, meeting his demand with her own to match.

"I have to have you," he murmured.

Katherine acquiesced his request, wanting him too, and forgetting her own misgivings of earlier let him push her over toward a settee. There was time to discuss what they were, whatever that may be. They could do that tomorrow, away from the ball and any eavesdropping matrons of the *ton*. Tonight, right now, she wanted to have him all to herself, love him as much as she adored him and show him that she was his, if only he'd ask.

The settee hit the back of her legs and she sat. Hamish didn't waste any time before bearing her down, hitching her skirts up about her waist, his hand sliding against her core in tantalising strokes.

"I cannot get enough of you," he said, his voice roughened with desire. He kneeled between her legs and ripped at his frontfalls, coming back over her and thrusting into her hard. They both moaned at the sheer delight of being together in this way. He kissed her hard, and she gasped as he pushed her toward a fast climax. They fit so perfectly well, and she shut her eyes as tears pricked behind her lids. She wouldn't become emotional over their joining, even if it was so very good. All that she'd hoped to have with a husband one day, back when she'd thought to marry.

His strokes deepened and with it the pleasure of their joining teased with exquisite torture. "Hamish, just there. Don't stop."

The whispered word 'never' tickled her ear and ecstasy rocked through her, hard and fast and she muffled her moan into the shoulder of his jacket. He took her without restraint then and with a muffled groan found his own pleasure within her.

The moment he did he stilled.

"What's wrong?" she asked, pulling her head back from his shoulder to look at him.

"I didn't pull out," he said, frowning. "Damn it, Katherine. I'm sorry."

She shook her head, dismissing the idea that the one time he'd made such an error would ever result in a baby. "I'm sure it'll be fine. Let us not needlessly worry unless we need to."

The fact that he hadn't mentioned that he'd marry her should the mistake result in a child, hurt. Hamish had come to mean so much to her. Did he feel the same? By his reaction she could only assume he hadn't come to feel for her as she did for him. For it had been many weeks since Katherine, without any doubt came to realize she loved him. With all her heart and would give anything for him to feel the same.

He moved off her, righting his clothes and she stood, doing the same, going over to a nearby mirror and fixing her hair. "I had better return to the ball. I shall see you again soon." Moving toward the door, he grabbed her arm, pulling her to stop.

Leaning down, Hamish kissed her with such tenderness that she pulled away and left without another word. Why she was so emotional made no sense, she was not normally a woman who succumbed to hysterics. She just needed some time, to think about what she would say to Hamish when she saw him again, but no matter what, if they were not going to have a future, then the liaison had to come to an end. The thought made her double over and she leaned against the wall, not wanting to even imagine a future without him. Why did she have to proposition him? Why did she have to know what lying with a man would be like? If only it wasn't going to be her heart that broke in two when he agreed to her fears and they parted as friends.

THE FOLLOWING DAY Katherine had been summoned to the Duchess of Athelby's for afternoon tea, but upon arrival found only Darcy and Cecilia present. Pleasure at having her friends to herself was soon replaced by the tempered looks they cast her upon arrival.

Katherine sat in the available wing back chair, folding her hands in her lap and wondered what was amiss. "You two are very glum this afternoon. Is there something wrong?"

Darcy poured the tea, throwing her a tentative smile before sitting down. Cecilia was quiet, contemplative and taking a sip of her tea then placed the cup on the linen covered table and met her eyes. "You were seen last night, in the music room, and not by us. Should it have been any one of us, as your friends we would've hidden any infraction you may have taken part in, but we cannot hide what is in today's gossip rag."

Thankfully Katherine was seated, for had she been standing her legs would've surely given out. She'd been seen? Oh, dear lord, which part had they seen? The kiss or the second act where Lord Leighton had pinned her upon the sofa and…Oh no…

She cringed, and picking up the paper, read the words that seemed to scream out at her, mocking and ripping her reputation to shreds. Harlot!

"Father reads this paper." Her heart skidded to a stop, her gown too tight, the room spun and distantly she heard Darcy call out for salts. Within a moment she was cast back to reality, but no sooner had that occurred the thought of what all of London knew, what they were thinking ricocheted through her mind.

She read the article a second time, not wanting to believe what was written in black and white.

A certain woman, with the initials of KM, from a social sphere several steps below that of the ton was seen frittering with a certain gentleman Lord L. The lady seen, in a most compromising position will not reconstruct her reputation from here, no matter how well her family have the ability since its their specialized trade.

"I'm RUINED. I should probably leave." Katherine stood, and Darcy reached out a hand, stopping her.

"You're not going anywhere. What happened last night, Katherine, we need to know. The duke has gone to fetch Lord Leighton as we speak, there are things we must do to try and salvage your reputation."

Katherine stood and walked to the decanter of whisky, pouring herself a glass, drinking it down before repeating it all again. Her father would be crushed to know she'd fallen. He would be livid, which was not a state that Katherine ever saw him in. And she'd done that to him. She'd embarrassed everyone including herself.

She met her friends' concerned eyes and sighed. "You know I wanted an affair with Lord Leighton, to experience a little of what you both have. I had resigned myself to never marry, never finding the man whom I loved and respected."

"That is not true, Kat. You're a beautiful woman and anyone would be honoured to marry you. If only you would let us seek you potential suitors," Cecilia said, taking her hand.

Katherine squeezed it a little before letting it go. Either way, her friend's words did not change what she knew to be true. Had she been desirable, attractive she would've married years ago. Her dowry was large, more than a lot of people imagined, but even that had not been tempting enough. Or too tempting and her only courtiers were fortune hunters. "Lord Leighton is famous for his blonde, goddess like women who have curves in all the right places. Beautiful skin, and sparking eyes. I may have pretty eyes, I will admit to that, but my hair is the colour of rats' fur."

"Katherine, that is absurd. Stop talking about yourself in such a way. I'll not allow it," the duchess declared, crossing her arms about her front.

"But you will allow it because it's the truth. The only reason why Lord Leighton and I were together was because he owed me a favour. Nothing more. I've come to realize that now."

The front door slammed and within a moment the front parlor door opened and in walked Lord Leighton and the Duke of Athelby. Hamish looked wretched, his hair askew and cravat laying untied about his neck.

The duke went to stand over beside a window, looking

out onto the street, and Hamish came over to her, kneeling beside her.

"Kat, I'm so sorry. I should never have allowed all that I have to happen between us, and now I've ruined you."

"You must fix this, Leighton. Make this right," the duke said, not looking at them.

"Right?" Hamish asked, frowning at the duke. "And how do you suppose I'd manage that?"

Heat bloomed on Katherine's cheeks and she stood, walking over to stand before the fire, suddenly chilled. "He means make it right by marrying me, Lord Leighton."

His lordship met her eyes, the horror on his features all that she needed to see to know her place. The little piece of her heart that hoped he may care for her, would wish to maybe marry her instead of continuing his bachelor ways shrivelled and died.

The shock and disappointment in Darcy and Cecilia's gaze made her understand more than ever before that he was only ever having fun. And it was her own fault, she'd offered herself as a prize, too ugly and thin to be worthy of love, too tarnished by trade, housed too far away from Mayfair to be suitable. She should've let Lord Leighton have his skull cracked open that night at the Inn. She should've walked away, but she hadn't. Because she'd known who he was and knew they had mutual friends, even if he wasn't aware.

"I must go," she said, walking to the door.

Lord Leighton crossed in front of her, blocking her way.

"Katherine, we will make this right. I shall not allow your reputation to be tarnished over something that cannot be proved."

She shook her head, not knowing that someone who had given her so much ecstasy only hours before could cause so much pain that she physically hurt. "Go to hell, Hamish. I want nothing from you."

"You will marry my friend, or I'll call you out," Cecilia said, standing and throwing her hands on her hips.

Katherine smiled in thanks, but she could never marry a man who did not want her.

"Thank you, Lia, but I wouldn't marry Lord Leighton now even if he asked?"

"Why not?" Hamish and Darcy demand in unison.

"I don't intend to marry at all and I can promise you that I would never marry a man who hesitated, promised all sorts of ways to fix the ruination of my reputation, all but the one way in which to fix it. Marriage. I knew when we were together from the first that it was a risk, but I was willing to take it for one night with you. I will not throw myself at your mercy, for a union with a man who does not care for me." Katherine dipped into a small curtsy and left, only making the front steps before tears broke free and her shoulders shook in despair.

He had not been falling in love with her as she had been with him. She'd been alone in that emotion. The stone pavement shivered before her and without warning, she ran for the small hedged garden that sat on either side of the door and cast up her accounts.

A woman she'd seen at a ball stopped and looked her nose down at Katherine. She pulled out her handkerchief. If her ruination hadn't been sealed by todays paper, vomiting in front of Lady Cavendish certainly put paid to that.

CHAPTER 14

Hamish returned home to his country estate, disinviting his friends to join him, friends that had rallied about Miss Martin, consoling her in her upset, her despair of being ruined. He'd left for his estate, the draw of the city no longer what it once was, and nor would it ever be again.

Katherine was lost to him, despised him, just as Marchioness of Aaron and the Duchess of Athelby did as well. With their scorn, their husbands also saw less of him, withholding their invitations to dinners at their homes.

He sat alone in his dining room and stared at the long, deserted table before him. After seeing Katherine leave him at the duke and duchess of Athelby's home, he'd been in such a blind state of panic that he'd not chased her. Instead, he'd listened to the duke rile at him over his atrocious behaviour.

It was all he could do not to scream back. He'd been honest from the start with Katherine, had tried to make her see that he could not promise anything, that he didn't wish for a wife or children. Other than that one time, he'd been so careful with her, not wanting her to have consequences from their times together.

All a cold comfort for the pain at not having seen her, of having no contact or knowing if she was well tore him in two. He picked up his wine and poured himself another glass. He'd thought that his time away from town, of having space and not seeing her would help him move on from their liaison.

He was a fool. If anything, his time away from Katherine only made him yearn more for her. Night after night he woke up in a cold sweat, not from want or desire, but simply concern, the knowledge that he was no longer privy to her whereabouts or if she was well. He should have chased after her. By doing nothing that day he may have severed any possibility of gaining back her affections.

Damn bloody fool! He muttered.

The door to the dining room opened and he glanced up, groaning when he realized who'd come to stay.

"Hello mother," he said, saluting her with his glass.

His mother stormed into the room. "How dare you! How dare you throw our family into such scandal. Having an affair with the woman who ran the rebuild of your home. I'm beyond disappointed." She whacked her gloves down on the table. "What do you have to say for yourself?"

Hamish shut his eyes and counted to ten, anything but to lose his temper. He wanted to lash out, and if his mother kept speaking to him in such a way she would be the recipient of his opinions.

"Miss Martin may not be titled or as well connected as us, but she's a lady and was raised as one. Do not speak ill of her."

"You know that she's ruined, that she is no longer

welcomed at any Society ball. I can expect such base actions from her, she is after all tarnished by trade, but you. You I expected much more from. To have been intimate with someone of such little connections is beyond the pale."

Hamish pushed back his chair and stood, throwing his napkin on the table. "Do not lecture me about how I live my life. And do not talk about Katherine in that way. I ruined her, I walked away from her and let her face the costs of our actions alone. If anyone should be derided, it is me, and the society that saw fit to judge her when it wasn't their damn business."

Shame washed over him that he'd left Katherine alone. He was a disgrace and he'd allowed his fear of losing her to get the better of him when she'd needed him most.

"What do I care what happens to the doxy? You, my son need to marry a woman of respectable birth and untarnished reputation as soon as possible."

Hamish knew his mother was hard, uncaring even, but this. This coldness and the disdain of others was beyond the pale. How could anyone be so heartless? "Do not speak to me of such things. I will not be marrying anyone of your choosing."

Her eyes darkened in temper and she slammed her fist down on the table. "You will do what I say for it is plainly clear that you're incapable of acting as a responsible adult."

He shook his head. "No mother."

She didn't reply, simply glared at him a moment. "Who then? Who are you going to marry, for you had better marry someone to fix this scandalous mess our family now finds themselves in. Society will forgive you your affairs with whores, but to sleep with an unmarried woman who is under the protection of the Duke of Athelby through friendship, they will not."

"I will marry Miss Martin if she'll have me, just as I should have done weeks ago." He would return to town and fight for her forgiveness. Even if he had to lay himself bare on her doorstep and beg for forgiveness. First thing in the morning he would return to town and secure a marriage license. He would also have the housekeeper prepare the countess's room for their new mistress.

He would make this right again. He would beg Katherine's forgiveness and marry her if she'd have him. The thought of how he had not said anything, simply stood in the duchess's parlor that day like a simpleton and allowed her to walk out of his life.

"I will not allow a builders daughter to be your bride."

Hamish started for the door. "Then I suggest you pack your things and move to the dower house, for I shall try until my last breath is spent to win back her love." For that was exactly what it was. Love. He loved her, and he would make it right again. In this, he could not fail. He would not fail Katherine again.

KATHERINE HEAVED into the bowl on her nightstand over and over again, the sickness had come on suddenly and every day now she had the nausea as a good morning present. But no mornings would ever be good again. Tomorrow she was traveling to a cottage on the duchess of Athelby's country estate where she would stay for the duration of her pregnancy and then after that…well, she wasn't even sure what would happen after that.

Her father had surprisingly supported her, listened to

her when she'd gone to him with her shame. He'd been a pillar of strength for her, and she would miss him when away.

A knock sounded on the door and she walked back to the bed, sitting on its side. "Enter," she said, taking the glass of water from the nightstand and having a sip.

"It's me, dearest. I'm sorry to disturb you, but you have a visitor." Darcy said.

"I cannot see anyone. Send them away." Katherine lay back on the bed, pulling the blankets up to her chin. If only she could hide away here forever.

She heard the door creak open further and then a voice she'd not expected or wished to hear again sounded at the threshold. "May I come in, Katherine?"

She bolted upright. "No," she gasped, "Get out of my room and my life."

The door closed, and she sighed, half in relief, half despair. In the moment when she'd needed him most three weeks ago he'd not chased after her, not tried to right his wrong the following day. Instead he'd hightailed it back to the country and left her to the wolves.

Bastard.

The bed dipped on the other side, and anger coursed through her veins when the door clicked shut. Obviously, Darcy approved of Lord Leighton coming to see her. Well, she did not so he could go the hell away.

"Katherine, while I know whatever I say will never be enough, I want you to know that I'm so sorry. I panicked. Marriage always leads to children and I could not bear that for you. Childbirth is such a risk, and I've already lost a sister to the vile undertaking that I could not risk your life in the same way."

She cringed, knowing what a useless apology this was.

When he found out that she was carrying his child she would watch him again hightail it out of London and this time she doubted she'd ever see him again.

"I love you. You're everything to me, since the moment we met you've drawn me into your goodness, your laughter and independence." The bed wobbled as he stood and came about to kneel at her side of the bed. He took her hands, kissing them quickly. "Marry me, please. Forgive me my sins and tell me that you're mine and I'm yours. Please, I cannot live without you a moment longer."

Tears prickled behind her lids and she sniffed. "You left me. You left me defenceless and alone. You turned away without a backward glance. I will never forgive you for that."

His pallor changed to a sickly grey at her words and she shuffled off the bed, the nausea back with a vengeance. Katherine heaved and the silence behind her was deafening in the room.

"You're pregnant, aren't you?"

Had the situation not been so dire, she would've laughed at the horror on his voice.

Katherine picked up a cloth from beside the bowl and wiped her face and mouth. "Aren't you smart to have worked that out. Now off you go, Lord Leighton. There is the door, let me watch you scuttle away like the coward you are."

He ran a hand through his hair, not moving.

Damn it, he needed to leave. The despair on his visage at her cutting words pulled at her emotions and she didn't want to feel anything for him anymore. Least of all feel sorry for him! He'd played *her* the fool, and she wouldn't have it, no matter that she still loved him. Loved him more than anything ever in her life, save for the babe now growing inside her.

"Please Katherine, hear me out. I couldn't marry you for I knew I couldn't deny you anything, even the wish to have children. I wanted to keep you safe, to spare you such a fate. It was wrong of me, I know that now. I allowed my fear, my grief to guide my reactions and I will never forgive myself for it. Please, don't send me away."

"Why are you here, my lord? I am not the type of woman you're famous for having a taste for. What does it matter that a woman from Cheapside does not accept your hand in marriage? If we marry, you will soon tire of me and seek comfort elsewhere. I'm not willing to risk my heart in such a way. If I ever marry it shall be for love, and above all else loyalty and respect. You, Lord Leighton are lacking on the last two virtues."

"Did you just admit to loving me?" he said, stepping toward her. "For if it is love that you feel for me, and love that I feel for you, then surely that is as good a place as any to rebuild our trust and respect?"

She turned away from him, hating that her body yearned for the man while her mind railed at his treachery. "No, it's not."

He came about and stood before her. "Yes, it is. It is exactly the right base on which to start a life together, the very best, for with love, there is nothing that can break such a bond." He kneeled before her, looking up to meet her gaze. "Marry me, Kat. Be my wife and countess. Allow me to give you children. I cannot promise not to fuss over you, to worry and ensure you have the best doctors around at all times, but I shall try and tamper my anxiety over the condition if only you'll be the next countess of Leighton."

He held up a small velvet box and opened it. Inside sat a ring with the roundest, largest diamond Katherine had ever seen. Her heart skipped a beat.

"Your trinkets will not win me, my lord," she said,

wanting to look away from him and his gift, and yet, she couldn't do it. Both were magnificent really. His lordship begging for her was something she simply would not allow to stop. Not yet at least.

"I am the complete opposite to what you desire. I'm not blonde, full figured with birthing hips. You'll tire of me, leave me to rot in the country like so many noble women while you go about Covent Garden and spread your seed about like farmers feeding chickens."

He grinned, and she had to admit, the analogy wasn't the best one she'd ever thought of.

"You're everything that I want I just didn't know it. To me, there is no one more beautiful, of mind, body and soul. Make me a better man and say yes. Say yes to me, please."

She raised her brow, wanting to let him stew a little, while she thought about it.

"Katherine, your answer?" he said after a time. "What will it be, Miss Martin?"

She pursed her lips, coming to kneel with him. She took the ring and pulled it out, inspecting it while her stomach did somersaults. Could she forgive him. Could she marry an Earl?

"Yes," she said, slipping the ring on her finger and admiring it. Yes, she could.

He pulled her into a fierce hug and she laughed as he kissed every inch of her cheeks, her nose, her lips. "I love you. So much. I love you so much it hurts to think I could've lost you."

She nodded, running her hand through his hair and realizing she'd missed this, missed them. "I love you too." Katherine swallowed not wanting to cry and yet, she found Hamish wiping away a stray tear off her cheek.

"We will marry tomorrow. I have a special license and

then by tomorrow night you will be safely ensconced at my estate Hollyvale in Kent. And there, my dear, we will start our life together, raise our children and enjoy our existence."

"That sounds simply perfect."

EPILOGUE

The day of their daughter's second birthday started with a thunderstorm and by afternoon the sun had come out. Much like the day of her birth. On that day, Lord Leighton had stormed about the house, yelling at everything, cursing God and anyone who came within visual contact of him, and then by afternoon, when Rose had been born, he was all calm again. The happiest and most relieved lord in all of England.

Katherine had forgiven him his outbursts that day. She knew what it had cost him emotionally to see her go through with the birth, the worry, the fear. He was not alone, giving birth to a child was not an easy thing to do, and at times she hadn't thought she was capable of following through. But a woman's body is a strong and powerful thing, and she had managed through it. And in a few short months she would manage it again.

She hoped it was a boy, if only so Hamish would have a daughter and son. Two perfect little cherubs that they would love and adore until their dying breath.

Katherine finished reading the little nursery book to

Rose, and set her on her feet, just as her papa entered the bedchamber.

"How is my little princess," he said, picking her up and kissing her cheek. "Happy birthday beautiful girl."

"Present," their daughter said, clapping her hands.

Katherine laughed, how quickly children learned what birthdays and Christmas meant.

"Present," Hamish said in mock surprise. "You wish for a present?"

Rose nodded, her eyes bright with expectation.

Hamish set her down and tapped her bottom, pushing her toward the window. "Look outside princess and you'll see your gift."

Katherine stood and walked Rose to the window, pulling back the curtain she grinned at what she saw being led about on the lawns. A little white pony, with a great big pink bow tied about its neck.

Rose squealed and turned about, running for the door as fast as her little, unbalanced legs would take her.

"I think she likes it," Katherine said, taking Hamish's hand and following Rose. Her nursemaid picked Rose up before she reached the stairs and together they all walked outside to see the new addition to the family.

"She's beautiful, Hamish. Rose already loves her."

"It's a filly, and is very placid, I made sure of that. I think it will make a suitable first horse for our daughter."

Katherine leaned up and kissed him, not caring that their staff were about, not that she ever did, not from the first day she'd become mistress of this great estate, and the many others he owned.

"Thank you, Katherine."

She frowned up at him. "Whatever do you mean? Why are you thanking me?"

He met her gaze, his serious of a sudden. "For this life.

Had I not met you, had I not been having the worst start of any season I'd ever partaken in, I would not have met you or been given the greatest gift of all, our child."

She clasped his jaw, rubbing her thumb across his cheek. "You too have given me more than I could ever wish for, so thank you too. We're equal in this, Hamish. Always have been."

He nodded and turned his attention back to their daughter. Katherine stayed where she was as Hamish lifted Rose onto the saddle and holding her, allowed the groom to walk them about the yard.

This, Katherine mused was what life was meant for, meant to be like. Total bliss with abundance of love. How wonderful that a woman of little beauty, social value and dirt beneath her gloved fingernails had been perfect for one of London's most revered rogues. Had been enough to tempt an Earl.

INTRODUCING... TO BEDEVIL A DUKE

Lords of London, Book 1

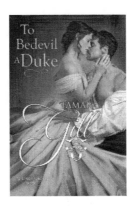

A Duke of many rules. A Lady of independence.

Since her cheating husband created a scandal by dying beneath his whore, Darcy de Merle is determined to enjoy widowhood, and refuses to mourn a man she grew to loathe. Setting the ton ablaze, Darcy holds a ball to re-launch herself into Society on the anniversary of his death.

Cameron, the Duke of Athelby plays by the rules. Always. He's lived through the terrible consequences of what revelry, carelessness, and lack of respect for one's social position can have on a family. So, when he sees Darcy de Merle skirting the boundaries of respectability, it is only right that he should remind her of the proper etiquette that she should adhere to.

Darcy refuses to allow another man to tell her what to do. When the Duke of Athelby chastises her at every turn, reminding her of her social failures, well, there is only one thing to be done about it...seduce the duke and show him there is more to life than the proper conventions set by the ton.

A battle of wills ensues where all bets are off, numerous rules are broken and love becomes the ultimate reward.

INTRODUCING... TO
MADDEN A MARQUESS

Lords of London, Book 2

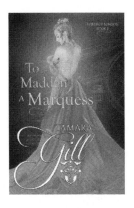

She saved his life, but can she save him from himself?

Hunter, Marquess of Aaron, has the ton fooled. Outwardly he's a gentleman of position, with good contacts, wealth and charm. Inwardly, he's a mess. His vice—drinking himself into a stupor most days—almost kills him when he steps in front of a hackney cab. His saviour, a most unlikely person, is an angel to gaze at, but with a tongue sharper than his sword cane.

Cecilia Smith dislikes idleness and waste. Had she been born male, she would already be working for her father's law firm. So, on a day when she was late for an important meeting at one of her many charities, she was not impressed by having to step in and save a foxed gentleman rogue from being run over.

When their social spheres collide, Hunter is both surprised and awed by the capable, beautiful Miss Smith. Cecilia, on the other hand, is left confused and not a little worried by her assumptions about the Marquess and his demons. It is anyone's guess whether these two people from different worlds can form one of their own...

INTRODUCING... TO VEX
A VISCOUNT

Lords of London, Book 4

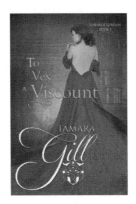

For the past six years, Miss Lizzie Doherty has had exactly zero proposals. Not because she isn't attractive, or from a good family, or doesn't have well-connected friends, but simply because she is poor. Or so the ton believe. Invited to a country house party on a stormy night,

her journey takes an unexpected turn when her driver delivers her to the wrong estate. Upon entering the home, she's soon masked and sworn to secrecy. Never has Lizzie ever experienced such an odd and intriguing event, so she plays along to see where the night will take her.

Lord Hugo, Viscount Wakely lives for sin, for anything scandalous, and for house parties that involve all of those things. At least he used to. But imagine his surprise when his good friends' ward, Miss Lizzie Doherty, an innocent and a successful debutante six years running, arrives at the last debauchery house party he'll attend. Or when an impromptu, scandalous kiss turns his life upside down.

Lizzie decides to stay for the week-long house party. Masks keep the guests' identities secret, but Lizzie would know Lord Hugo Wakely anywhere. And that one impromptu, scandalous kiss tells her that he is the Viscount for her…he just doesn't know it yet.

INTRODUCING... TO DARE A DUCHESS

Lords of London, Book 5

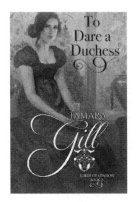

After five long years trapped in the country, newly widowed Nina Granville, Duchess of Exeter, has returned to town to start over. But it was here she committed an indiscretion—one stolen night of pleasure—that would threaten all she holds dear if revealed.

Byron always loved Nina from afar—until the house party that turned his world upside down. Guilt saw him flee England's shores, and Nina wed to a man old enough to be her grandfather, but now the handsome rogue is back... and ready to claim what is his.

Yet Nina has kept a secret from Byron, one that could threaten their sizzling attraction and sever their long-standing friendship forever. With Byron's brother determined to reveal the truth, Nina must use her power in the ton to ensure her secret is kept safe. Even at the expense of love...

INTRODUCING... TO MARRY A MARCHIONESS

Lords of London, Book 6

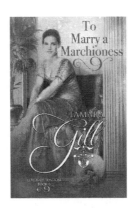

The sixth book in the bestselling
Lords of London series!
Available 03/19/2019

FEED AN AUTHOR, LEAVE A REVIEW

If you enjoyed TO TEMPT AN EARL, and would like to tell other readers your thoughts on the book, then please consider leaving a review at your preferred online bookstore or Goodreads.

ALSO BY TAMARA GILL

ONLY A DUKE WILL DO

ONLY A VISCOUNT WILL DO

A Time Traveler's Highland Love Series

TO CONQUER A SCOT

TO SAVE A SAVAGE SCOT

Daughters Of The Gods Series

DAUGHTERS OF THE GODS - SERIES BUNDLE

BANISHED-GUARDIAN-FALLEN

ABOUT THE AUTHOR

Tamara is an Australian author who grew up in an old mining town in country South Australia, where her love of history was founded. So much so, she made her darling husband travel to the UK for their honeymoon, where she dragged him from one historical monument and castle to another.

A mother of three, her two little gentleman in the making, a future lady (she hopes) and a part-time job keep her busy in the real world, but whenever she gets a moment's peace she loves to write romance novels in an array of genres, including regency, medieval and time travel.

www.tamaragill.com
tamaragillauthor@gmail.com